THE EXCHANGE

Books by Graham Joyce

Dreamside
Dark Sister
House of Lost Dreams
Requiem
The Tooth Fairy
Spiderbite
The Stormwatcher
Indigo
Leningrad Nights (contributor)
Smoking Poppy
The Facts of Life
TWOC: Taken Without Owner's Consent
The Limits of Enchantment
Black Dust (short stories)
The Exchange

THE EXCHANGE

GRAHAM JOYCE

VIKING

VIKING
Published by Penguin Group
Penguin Group (USA) Inc., 345 Hudson Street, New York, New York 10014, U.S.A.
Penguin Group (Canada), 90 Eglinton Avenue East, Suite 700, Toronto, Ontario, Canada M4P 2Y3 (a division of Pearson Penguin Canada Inc.)
Penguin Books Ltd, 80 Strand, London WC2R 0RL, England
Penguin Ireland, 25 St Stephen's Green, Dublin 2, Ireland (a division of Penguin Books Ltd)
Penguin Group (Australia), 250 Camberwell Road, Camberwell, Victoria 3124, Australia (a division of Pearson Australia Group Pty Ltd)
Penguin Books India Pvt Ltd, 11 Community Centre, Panchsheel Park, New Delhi—110 017, India
Penguin Group (NZ), 67 Apollo Drive, Rosedale, North Shore 0632, New Zealand (a division of Pearson New Zealand Ltd.)
Penguin Books (South Africa) (Pty) Ltd, 24 Sturdee Avenue, Rosebank, Johannesburg 2196, South Africa

Penguin Books Ltd, Registered Offices: 80 Strand, London WC2R 0RL, England

Originally published in the United Kingdom by Faber & Faber as *Do the Creepy Thing*, 2007
First published in the United States of America by Viking, a member of Penguin Group (USA) Inc., 2008

1 3 5 7 9 10 8 6 4 2

LIBRARY OF CONGRESS CATALOGING-IN-PUBLICATION DATA
Joyce, Graham.
The exchange / by Graham Joyce.
p. cm.
Summary: While fourteen-year-old Caz and her best friend creep through a stranger's home late one night, the elderly resident awakens and clamps onto Caz's wrist a silver bracelet which, overnight, turns into a tattoo that holds a curse, and as Caz's life disintegrates around her, she must find a way of lifting the curse—or at least understanding its power.
ISBN: 978-0-670-06207-2
[1. Blessing and cursing—Fiction. 2. Supernatural—Fiction. 3. Conduct of life—Fiction. 4. Dating (Social customs)—Fiction. 5. Tattooing—Fiction. 6. Single-parent families—Fiction.] I. Title.
PZ7.J827Exc 2008
[Fic]—dc22
2007032160

Printed in U.S.A. Set in Book Antiqua Book design by Jim Hoover

to my niece,
Samantha Joyce

CONTENTS

THE EXCHANGE

CHAPTER ONE
Creepy, Interrupted

CAZ LIVES ABOUT ten minutes' walk from the centre of town. Five minutes if you jog, but who the hell wants to jog? She also lives close enough to the river for the blue mists of spring and the grey fogs of autumn to haul themselves out of the water, roll along the bank, climb over the back-yard wall, and reach cold, damp fingers into the house where she lives alone with her mum.

Just two girls together. That's the way it has been since her dad ran off with the teenage babysitter when Caz was nine. "Actually, it's a relief," is what Caz's mum said at the time. But the smart house on the hill got sold and Caz and her mum moved into an old, brick, terraced property. The wooden window frames are rotten and the doors are drafty. Damp mould peppers one wall of the kitchen.

If Caz's mother was a drunk, or a debt-head, or just a nasty-bitch-in-general, then it would be easy to blame her for some of the things Caz gets up to. The old *I-didn't-have-a-normal-childhood* defence. The *broken-home* plea. The *understandable-with-my-background* line of argument. But Caz's mother isn't, and so Caz can't, and anyway Caz wouldn't.

Truth is, Caz's mother is nice as pie. Nice as pecan-with-fresh-cream pie. Actually, she is better than any kind of pie. She takes no shit, but ever since she first started living alone with Caz she's kept her head up, worked hard to keep house for the two of them, been a friend to Caz as well as a mother, and gone without things herself so that Caz can have the very best of what is available.

So who is Caz going to blame for her own behaviour? That's right, no one but herself.

If you were the kind of person who held small things against people, here is just about all you could say against Caz's mum: she sleeps like a pig. Snores like one, too. In fact her snoring is like the sound of someone driving a whole herd of unruly pigs to market. This in itself is not a *bad* thing. People don't snore out of badness, and they don't sleep heavily out of meanness, either. Her sleeping just happens to be the element that enables Caz to get up to the things she does.

The things she shouldn't get up to.

It's the pills. The tranquillisers Caz's mum takes for depression. She seems to have been depressed for as long as Caz can remember: even before Dad ran off. Okay, so the little pills help with the mood swings, but they put her mum in a kind of fog. And when she's not in a fog she's sleeping deep. Caz wonders if fogging and sleeping and snoring through life isn't more depressing than depression itself.

But the pills are probably what made it all happen. If there hadn't been the pills, Caz's mum wouldn't have been so given over to slumber. If she hadn't been lost in her underwater cavern of sleep, Caz wouldn't have been out at night doing the Creepy Thing.

Caz has tested her mum. It is possible to slam doors, clang saucepans, and ring bells in her ear without her once stirring. When her mum is *gone*, she is *gone*, making it possible for Caz to take the key from the hook where it hangs in the hall and let herself out the door after midnight, safe in the knowledge that her mum will sleep soundly, unreachable as an astronaut orbiting the earth. Perhaps if Caz's mother had been one of those people who jerk themselves awake at the very moment a pin, having sliced through the air, thuds and wobbles like a javelin as it impales the fibres of the carpet, things would be different. But no.

And while astronauts and dreamers are in high places, other people can be in low places. Not that it has ever been Caz's intention to be the sort of person who would break into people's houses with burglary in mind.

"That," she tells Lucy, her companion on these jaunts, "is such a *chavvy* thing to do."

"You calling me a *chav*?" Lucy bridles. Lucy has yellow-brown eyes that flare like a struck match when something is said to upset her.

"No, I didn't say you *were* one, I said breaking into people's houses is one thing but stealing is another."

"Well? Not as if we're nicking stuff, is it?"

Caz just looks at Lucy. In her case—Caz's case—it is true, because she's never stolen anything; in Lucy's case, it isn't always. Once when they were out Lucy had pocketed a wedding ring and a gold necklace, which she'd only revealed later. The girls had had a fight over the matter. Not a hair-pulling, eye-gouging, face-scratching kind of fight, but nasty things were said on both sides. Caz went so far as to say that if Lucy didn't return the jewellery, then the friendship was over. Lucy refused and threw the ring and necklace into the gutter, from where Caz retrieved them. She took the gold items back to the house in the dead of night and dropped them through the letterbox.

Because, as Lucy said, it's not as if they are thieves. They aren't there to rob old people. They are just there to . . . *do the Creepy Thing.*

Lucy learned how to break into a house from a boyfriend called Jamie, the kind of lad who kept his mouth wide open just to breathe; the kind Caz would call a *chav.* Lucy quickly showed Caz, who already knew at least three better ways to do it. Caz wasn't interested in housebreaking. It was just that she'd often been in a position where she'd had to force an entry into her own house, or even her old house on the hill shortly after they'd vacated it. Convinced she'd left in a cupboard a tiny velvet pouch containing her milk teeth, she went back there and broke in before the new owners arrived. She didn't find anything, but she did get a thrill from poking around the place.

Another time, in their current house, when she'd gone

to collect the milk from the doorstep, a sudden breeze had slammed the door shut behind her, leaving her shivering in her pyjamas. Mum was at work. She found that the rotting Victorian sash windows were no more difficult to get past than a piece of crumbling biscuit. After that experience, Caz went round all the windows with a power drill, some brackets, and a set of screws, adding a bit of security to the place.

After all, you never knew who was about.

But the point, as far as Caz is concerned, isn't to break in and knock off jewellery and a dusty old DVD player. The point about doing the Creepy Thing is to get in silently, while the occupants are in the house at the time. While the occupants are fast asleep.

And right now it's Lucy's turn.

They've chosen an old man's house: they always choose old people's houses, on the basis that a pensioner might not be so nimble in pursuit if a quick getaway is required. It's a brick terraced house with a side alley offering a gate into a back yard. Entering via a sash window was child's play, and they're already upstairs and going for it.

A crack in the closed curtains lets in just enough silver moonlight for Caz, crouched behind the half-open bedroom door, to see. She is on her toes, ready to make a bolt for it if the old man wakes up. Lucy is halfway across the room, delicately moving along the carpet. The snores coming from the figure under the bedclothes are not like her mother's snores. This sounds like someone lazily drawing a bow-saw across a plank of wood. Caz's heart knocks in her rib cage. In her mind, she is already down the stairs and out the door. She knows she shouldn't be there, but at moments like this she feels like she's hanging out of the door of an aeroplane with the wind blowing through her hair. She feels alive, in every cell of her body. The few feet of darkness of the room between her and the sleeping man is the drop through thin air. Escape is the parachute.

Caz has been holding her breath, but now she lets herself breathe. The room stinks of something she can't quite identify. Like toffee. Or maybe Marmite. Whatever it is, she associates it with the old man in the bed. She can see part of a bald head and a striped pyjama sleeve where the old man has his arm thrown out from under the covers. On a bedside table, next to a silver-framed photograph of an old lady with spectacles and a blue-rinse, a bedside clock ticks loudly. It's just after one o'clock. A glass of water stands next to the clock, along with two little brown bottles of pills.

Lucy is making good but slow progress across the carpet when, right under her foot, a floorboard creaks. It's a ripping noise, so loud it seems to split the damp air and stop the clock. Without waiting for Lucy, Caz spins on her heels and bolts down the stairs. They've left the door ajar, but before reaching it she can feel Lucy breathing hard at the back of her neck.

They're out and running.

They don't look back as they hurtle down the street

into the night. They have no idea if the old man is following. The rule is: you don't look back.

They fly down the street, lungs cracking, trying to stick to the shadows from the orange halogen streetlamps. Caz's legs turn to slush. Lucy, faster, overtakes her, thumping her hard on the shoulder as she goes past.

"Prat! You prat!"

They bullet across a scrap of wasteland and scramble through a gap in the hedge, escaping from there into the park by the river. They don't stop running until they reach the old bandstand. Only then do they collapse on each other, hyperventilating, trying to gulp air back into their painful lungs.

"I'm not doing that again," wheezes Caz.

"I'd have been all right! You panicked. You're useless!" Lucy manages.

"He was awake! The old bugger was awake!"

"He wasn't!"

"I bet he is now."

And at last the gasping for breath turns to laughter. They both laugh so hard their ribs threaten to crack. It's that kind that sucks all the breath out of your lungs. It's the kind of laughter that squeezes the snot from your nose. It drains all the strength from their knees. Dangerous laughter. You can stay high for a week on that kind of dangerous laughter.

That's why they do it. To get a blast of that dangerous, wicked laughter.

At last Lucy shakes her head and looks round the bandstand floor for a place to sit. It isn't too clean as hideouts go. Kids have made fires there. She finds a plank of wood and drags it across the floor before lowering her bum onto it, her head in her hands and her long silky black hair falling all over her face as she recovers herself.

It's a while before Caz can speak. When she does, she says, "I'm going home."

"What? You're joking!" Lucy would stay out all night if she could find someone to stay with her.

"What if he's called the police? We might get picked up. I'm going."

"He wasn't even awake!"

But Caz is out of the bandstand and heading for the path that runs by the river. From there a path will take her to the back gate of her house on Otter Street. She doesn't even look over her shoulder. She doesn't have to: she knows Lucy will follow. And anyway, she knows her situation is different from Lucy's. Lucy's mum wouldn't even care if she knew she was out on the tiles, whereas Caz's—if she ever woke up to discover her daughter missing—would go ape.

"I'll see you in school tomorrow," Caz tells Lucy.

CHAPTER TWO

I Don't Do Youth Clubs

ALL DAY AT school, Lucy is in a sulk. A mysterious sulk. Caz isn't allowed to know what the sulk might be about, though she can guess. It's just something Lucy refuses to talk about.

This is the way Lucy sulks: she puffs her huffs full of wind and long, drawn-out sighs and low groans and moans, like a church organ. She folds her arms and looks the other way, avoiding eye contact with Caz. She lets her luscious bottom lip jut out. If asked a direct question, she shrugs. She's a bloody pain, is sulky Lucy, and Caz says so.

"You can't be on your period," Caz says, "because you were sulky and moody last week. And the week before that, come to think of it. And the week before that. And you'll be sulky next week, too."

Lucy's eyes flare, but she isn't going to be drawn that easily. She rubs her back against the brick wall of the new school gymnasium and looks the other way. Caz does likewise. Only Caz can't seem to push her bottom lip out quite as far as can Lucy.

They're an odd couple. According to Caz, there are three groups of girls: text-teenies, makeup-dollies, and gym-janes. The first group dedicate all day to texting each other: *how r u? good how r u? good how r u? still good how r u?* The second spend their time at school trying to put on slap and then scrubbing it off before getting caught. The third group are lost in a puzzling world of trampolines and handsprings, such that whenever one walks by, Caz feels compelled to say, *"Boing!"*

In fact Caz won't even carry a mobile phone, so contemptuous is she of the art, much to Lucy's disgust. But neither Caz nor Lucy fit in with any of these groups, and for that reason they bond, even though they exasperate each other and spend much of their time being in some kind of a dark mood with the other.

A little farther along the gym wall a kid is being roughed up. Lucy and Caz watch, barely interested, though it distracts them from having to speak to each other. It's just routine bullying. A boy called Luke Prospect, otherwise known as Lord Swot-a-Lot, is having his schoolbag thrown around again. The bullies, four of them, snatch Luke's glasses and try them on, pretending to walk blindly into the gym wall. They rifle his bag, slinging his books to the ground. It's the sort of thing that could last two minutes or the full half hour.

Until Mark Morris and Conrad Williams happen along, and take an interest in the bullying. And because Mark and Conrad, each two years older than the girls, are amongst the hottest guys in the school, Caz and Lucy unfold their arms and pay attention.

Mark intercepts the flying bag by simply reaching up a hand and plucking it out of the air. Conrad grabs back the glasses and returns them to Luke Prospect, gently hooking the frames around the bullied boy's ears. The four bullies stop dead. Then one of them makes to grab the bag again, but Mark puts himself between Luke and the bullies.

"Why you sticking your noses in?" snarls the chief bully, a copper-haired boy with a curling lip.

Mark, a tall, thin boy with brown hair and dark eyes, says nothing. He just folds his arms and smiles.

"You wanna be careful, Mark," mouths another of the bullies, a youth with a shaved head. "You might be taking on more than you can handle."

Mark's friend Conrad, a boy with smooth, dark skin the colour of milky coffee, steps towards Mark and drapes his hand across his friend's shoulder. He just smiles, too, and, like Mark, says nothing. It's a gesture that declares: *Two against four and what are you going to do about it?*

For a few seconds there is a stand-off. Luke makes himself busy, quickly seizing those books that were thrown on the floor. Then the four bullies turn on their heels. As they leave, one of them makes some dirty racial remark aimed at Conrad. But it's a cowardly over-the-shoulder shot, too low to tell which of them has said it.

Conrad just blinks, watching their disappearing backs. He gives a tiny shake of his head.

"Thanks," says Luke.

"One you owe us," says Mark.

Luke scuttles away in the opposite direction of the bullies.

"See that?" whispers Caz. "They didn't say a single word."

Mark and Conrad head away from the scene and towards the girls. Caz and Lucy can't help themselves. They've admired these boys from afar, but never before have they had an opportunity to speak with them. Caz flicks at her hair. Lucy moistens her lips.

"Hi Mark," says Lucy, with a pleasant ring to her voice.

"Hi Mark, hi Conrad," says Caz, in a lovely singsong accent.

"Hi Conrad," says Lucy, in a kind of melody.

"Ffff," goes Mark.

"Drrr," goes Conrad.

These are of course not real words that the boys make, but sounds. Perhaps if the girls were sixteen and not fourteen, they might be worthy of the gift of proper speech in response to their greeting. But it seems they are not, and the boys pass by, not having ignored the girls, but not having acknowledged them, either.

Except for this small thing: Mark glances up at the clouded blue sky, just for a second, as if checking out the flight of a passing bird, or maybe checking out nothing at all. It's no more than a moment of distraction, in which he can't help shifting his fleeting look from the sky to Caz's cornflower-blue eyes. Just a darting glance. A flicker of eye contact. Nothing. Or maybe something.

As soon as the boys have passed beyond the line of vision, a sparkle fades in the girls' eyes. Lucy folds her arms again, and out come the bottom lips. Then the bell goes, to indicate that lunch break is over.

Caz waits to see if her friend is going to climb out of her mood. After a couple of minutes, it's clear that Lucy will not.

"Well, sod you then," says Caz, and off she goes to her Information Technology lesson.

Normally at the end of the school day Caz would wait for her friend, and they would make the dawdling walk home together, eventually peeling off from each other at the abandoned grey-brick church of St Osburgh's. But Lucy's sulks have been one too many, so she cuts through the scrum of kids at the school gates and heads off alone.

Not that she gets very far on her own. She immediately senses someone hurrying behind here. She thinks it's Lucy, but it's a boy's voice who asks her, "Shway goan?"

Caz stops dead. "Pardon?"

There's a pause followed by a tiny cough. "I said which way you going?"

Caz is amazed at two things. Firstly the stupidity of the question. It should be obvious that she is going in the direction in which she is walking. She wants to let fly with her normal sarcasm, the sort she pumps at people like rounds from a double-barrelled shotgun. But she can't. Because the boy is Mark Morris.

Mark Morris! Mark who sticks up for geeks. Mark who stands up against bullies. Mark whom she tried to speak to at lunchtime and who answered with a moment's eye contact! Mark who is only the best-looking boy in the school, or who would be if only he could find a better pair of shoes! Mark who *never* speaks to her, because he's sixteen and she's fourteen! That Mark!

And he's blushing.

Caz looks him in the eye and rolls her top lip over her bottom lip, which she knows will make her look weird. But it's a habit she's developed to stop herself saying all those sarcastic things which just come spilling out if she's not careful. And now she's trapped. Caught between saying something with that chain-saw mouth of hers and looking mean; or saying nothing and looking dumb.

Dumb wins out. She points forward, a little pinky jabbing the air in front of her.

"Walk with you then?" Mark says.

It's a question. She has to tell herself it's a question: *He's asking if he can walk with me.* She wants to speak, to say something cool: *Yeah, sure, why not?* But her tongue sticks to the roof of her mouth. A smile she just hates has twisted her mouth. And *oh no* she feels a matching blush filling up her face, starting from the neck, reaching to the very tips of her ears and then spreading up and over her face like a rash to the very roots of her hair. This is no ordinary flush, this is like a tidal wave of blackcurrant juice miraculously refilling the bottle. She looks away, to hide the juice.

Dismayed, he falls back half a step, taking this as a kind of rejection.

"Where do you live?" she hears herself say.

"Hillfields," he says, quickening his step, falling in with her again.

It's in the very opposite direction. She can't look him in the eye now. Not with all these fruit blenders going off in her face. "So you're going the wrong way," she says.

"Yeah." He laughs. "Yeah. I'll have to turn round in a bit."

They walk for a while in silence. She tries to look at him from the corner of her eye while keeping her attention directed forward. It's not easy. It isn't easy at all. She can tell he's not comfortable, though he's trying to look cool. He has his hands in his pockets and his head is tilted back a fraction too far. Like he doesn't care. Like he just happens to walk the wrong way home from school every day. Like, yeah. But it's all right, because at least the blackcurrant juice is starting to drain from her face. At least she feels her pale features returning to her.

Then he says, as though it's nothing, as if it is nothing at all, like completely nothing, "Wanna go out on a date?"

Caz looks at the ground. She runs a hand through her hair. "Huh?"

"Well?"

"Go out where?"

"Anywhere."

Caz shrugs. She hitches her canvas schoolbag higher on her shoulder.

"How about tonight?" he says.

A car speeds past, tooting the horn, but not at them. Or maybe it was at them. Some drivers, older guys, seem to think it's fun to toot the horn at schoolgirls who wear short skirts. They both turn and look at the speeding car. It fills the moment.

"Okay," she says, coming to her senses. "Do you know the bandstand in Abbey Park? By the river?"

"Yeah. Seven o'clock?"

"Not seven. Twelve. Midnight."

Mark's face becomes a tangled knot. His eyebrows knit. A deep crease appears above the bridge of his nose. His mouth twists at the corner, like someone caught his lip with a fish hook and is tugging the line. "Midnight? Are you crazy?"

"Please yourself. I don't do Youth Clubs."

"Huh? I don't do Youth Clubs, either. But midnight . . . wow."

They've reached the street corner, where the grey, gloomy, and almost derelict spire of the church of St Osburgh's scowls down at them. Caz sees her chance to get away.

"I'll be there," she says. "Midnight."

She peels off, leaving him standing on the corner, baffled, his hands in his pockets, staring after her. That Mark Morris.

CHAPTER THREE
Too Sexy for a First Date

"YOU LOOK TIRED, Caroline," says Helen. "Are you getting enough sleep?" Helen is Caz's mum. She wears her hair long and is still pretty enough, but she has allowed two vertical creases to make a permanent home between her eyebrows. Whenever she asks a question like this, the creases get deeper and darker. Her face is puffed from the Loxetine pills. Helen used to take Prozac, but she couldn't sleep, so her doctor switched her to Loxetine antidepressants. Now she sleeps so well she's come to believe that sleep is the answer to all the world's ills: *If only people would sleep more.*

"I'm sleeping fine," Caz says, winding spaghetti onto a spoon with her fork. Thursdays is always spaghetti Bolognese, but for some reason Helen isn't eating tonight. She's set only one plate, for Caz. Though she sits down at the table, she says she's not hungry.

Helen reaches across the table and tenderly parks a stray lock of hair behind Caz's ear. "You've got bags under your eyes. It's only old trouts like me who should have bags under their eyes."

"You're not an old trout."

"I've got pouches you could put money in. And crow's-feet lines round my eyes."

"Smile lines, Mum."

Helen laughs. It's a tinkly laugh, not a real laugh. It is true, she does have lines round her eyes, and it's also true they are smile lines. They crinkle when she laughs. Helen laughs a lot, but she also has a habit of *staring*. And when Caz catches Helen staring, she thinks that even the smile lines can't stop her from looking sad.

Then Helen drops her bombshell. "I'm going out."

Caz drops her fork. It splashes Bolognese sauce across the table. "What?"

"You don't mind, do you?"

"But you never go out!"

This isn't entirely true. Helen goes out on every other Friday with her sister to the cinema, and once a week during term time she attends a Tuesday evening salsa dance class at Caz's school. What Caz means is that her mother never goes out beyond a fixed schedule. "Well, I am tonight."

"Who are you going out with?"

"I'm going salsa dancing."

Caz smells something fishy. She hasn't asked her mother what she is doing, she's asked her *who* she is doing it with. She picks up her fork and begins eating again. But she barely takes her eyes off her mother.

"You've got a boyfriend!" Caz shouts triumphantly.

"Oh, for God's sake!" Helen exclaims, standing up and turning her back.

"You have, haven't you?"

"Have you finished with your plate?"

"Don't get embarrassed, Mum!"

"I am *not* embarrassed. And he's not a bloody boyfriend. Give me that plate!"

"You'd better make sure you use a condom," Caz says. Only six months earlier, Helen had told Caz all about condoms and about trouble with boyfriends. "We don't want you bringing trouble back here."

"Right," Helen shouts, ignoring the crack about a condom. "You clear up. I'm going upstairs to have a bath and get ready."

She is already halfway upstairs. Caz chases her, but only as far as the foot of the stairs. She wants to taunt her a bit more, find out a few things about this man. But she lets her mother go. She knows Helen can't handle it. She is being teased by her fourteen-year-old daughter and she just can't handle it.

Caz sits downstairs while her mother soaks in the bath. The television flickers in front of her, but she isn't watching it. The programmes seem to be junk fillers between the junk advertising. It's like having a fire to stare into: mesmerising but empty.

She is thinking about Mark. Caz told Mark that she'd see him at midnight, confident in the knowledge that her mum would be dozing in the land of Nod by ten thirty. Now mum is going out, and since she's probably fibbing about salsa dancing, if she stays out until pub closing time, won't get back until between eleven thirty and midnight.

Caz doesn't mind about her mum going out. In fact, she thinks it would be good for her to go and have some fun. She's often wondered what would happen if her mother came back with a boyfriend, though in Caz's fantasies they are always super-rich film stars or rock musicians who whisk them off to another life in the sun.

The reality would of course be different. She's teased her mum about using condoms, but she doesn't like to think about it too much. One day Helen had trapped her in her bedroom and produced a box of condoms. Caz had looked at it as if it were a smoking bomb. Her mum had actually unwrapped one of them and waved it under Caz's nose saying, "Caz, this is the difference between stupid people and smart people."

Not that Caz has ever come close to having sex with anyone. She's snogged a couple of boys, let them touch her breasts, but has never wanted it to go much further than that. When she thinks about Mark Morris, if he has his shirt off, he always has his trousers on. She wonders if he will show up at the bandstand that night. She can imagine him standing around waiting, shivering without a shirt, with the mist streaming off the river.

"What do you think?" Helen asks her. Her hair is still wet but she's slipped on a clingy black satin dress.

Too sexy for a first date, Caz thinks. "It looks good."

"You sure?"

"I don't know, Mum! Why are you asking me?"

"You don't think it's too . . ."

"Too what? You won't even tell me where you're going: how can I tell you if it's too anything?"

"Oh, all right, dammit! We're only going to a vegetarian restaurant."

We confirms it. Unless Helen is taking the gerbil out with her. But Caz doesn't respond. Instead she pretends to be engrossed in junk TV. "What time will you be back?" she asks casually.

Helen has found a towel and is drying her hair. "Not late. But don't wait up."

"Nice perfume," Caz says. "Did you use the whole bottle?"

As it happens, Helen is back in the house a little after ten. Caz, lazing on the sofa, hears a car draw up in the street outside and then hears her mother's heels tottering up the path. Caz goes to the window and opens a curtain. The car still has its engine running and exhaust fumes billow in the damp air. The courtesy light in the car winks off and though Caz can see the outline of the driver, she can't make out his features.

When Helen gets inside she says, "Come away from the window! What are you doing?"

"Trying to get a look at him. Is he coming in?"

"No. I've told him I'll lend him a book. Have you seen that book I was reading?"

"You haven't finished it yet!"

"Who cares? Help me find the damn book!"

Caz finds the paperback behind a cushion and hands it over. "Why won't he come in?"

"Shy," Helen says, grabbing the book. "And I don't blame him with you hanging out the window gawping."

"I'm not gawping!"

"You are! You're gawping. I looked up and saw your face in the window like a Halloween pumpkin." Helen checks her hair in the mirror, pats it right, pats it left, as if that's going to help. She's gone.

Caz skips back to the window to watch her mother totter down the path to open the passenger door. The courtesy light comes on again, but this time Helen is blocking Caz's view. After a moment, Helen closes the door and the car drives off. Helen waves.

Back inside, Helen smooths her hands across her dress. "Well. That was a nice evening."

"You're back early," Caz says.

"Yes. He likes an early night."

"Why didn't you bring him inside?"

"What, so you could stare at him? Anyway, he's quite shy."

Quite shy, thought Caz. *Vegetarian. Likes an early night.* "Not exactly rock and roll, is he?"

"What? You do say ridiculous things, Caroline. Know what? I'm starving. Do you want something to eat?"

"You've just been to a restaurant, Mum."

"I know, but I was so nervous I hardly ate a bite."

Helen rustles up a supper, talking constantly but somehow without saying anything. Caz knows there is something odd going on. The pitch of her mother's voice is just a tiny bit too high. Of course it could be put down to the excitement of her "date," but Caz feels that there is more. Any of her questions about the man Helen spent the evening with are deflected. Caz can't even get a name out of her mother.

But pretty soon her mum is yawning, and when Helen does finally go to bed, it leaves just about enough time for Caz to make her meeting with Mark at the bandstand. But she doesn't go.

He's not going to be there. She knows it.

CHAPTER FOUR

Say Nothing About Saying Nothing

"I MEAN, WHAT do you do there anyway?"

It's Mark Morris after school. Caz has been waiting for him, her legs crossed at the ankles, leaning her back against the brick wall at the school gates, making it seem as though she is hanging around for someone else, when really she has been waiting for him alone. Not that he would know. Not that she makes any kind of eye contact with him. Not that she so much as twitches a pretty eyebrow. But it is him she has in her rifle-sights.

Oh, yes.

She doesn't even look at him to answer this question. Just stares dead ahead at the frothing tide of kids bobbing past in their navy blue school uniforms. Then, at the moment when he thinks he's not going to get an answer at all, she says, "So how come you weren't there?"

He hitches his rucksack higher on his shoulder. "Had one or two other things to do."

Caz turns her head to look at him for the first time. She holds his gaze for a moment. He blinks. She looks away. "Oh, yeah?"

He laughs. "I bet you weren't even there yourself at midnight."

Caz shrugs.

He can't think what to say next, but at the same time he can't seem to tear himself away. He scrapes the ground with the sole of his shoe, like a pony hoofing the paddock field. He looks up at her. He looks away. Just when Caz thinks this hopeless conversation is going really well, trouble arrives.

And it arrives in the form of Lucy.

Lucy doesn't even seem to notice Mark's presence. With her white blouse untucked from her waist and her big hair flying out behind her, she arrives like a gusting high wind. She puts her nose two centimetres away from Caz's nose and says, "Where have you been all day?"

Her words splash on Caz like a wave of seawater on a rock. Caz's ice-blue eyes gaze steadily back into Lucy's hot sand-brown eyes. Caz notices a tiny cut, maybe like a cut a belt buckle might make, near her friend's hairline, but as is their rule she says nothing about it. She tries not to smile at Lucy's question. "School."

"You know what I mean. Have you been avoiding me?"

"I haven't been avoiding you."

Lucy takes a step to the side and folds her arms, incredibly tightly. Looking away from Caz's cool gaze, she spots Mark. "You don't go around avoiding your best friend, do you?"

Mark, taking the furious question to be directed at him, says, "No. You don't."

"I'm not talking to you!" Lucy snaps.

"Look," says Caz, "I haven't been avoiding you. Okay?"

Lucy relaxes. She unfolds her arms, as if to say, *That's all right then*. Her brown eyes soften and a sweet smile settles on her lips. She leans against the wall, next to Caz. The wind has gone. The water is calm. Just like that. She looks at Mark again. "What are you talking about, anyway?"

Mark says, "Are you talking to me? Am I allowed to speak?"

"Yes, you're allowed to speak," Lucy says.

"Good," says Mark. "Only I didn't want to get shouted at again."

"No," Lucy says sweetly, "you won't get shouted at."

"I was just asking what you do. You know, when you go out at night?"

"What?" Lucy says. "What?"

Caz has already started to walk away. As if, all along, she'd just been waiting for Lucy to come before going home. The other two follow her.

"Like last night," Mark says. "What did you get up to at midnight? I want to know."

Lucy looks at Caz. Caz closes her eyes for a moment. She knows Lucy would have been there, at the bandstand at midnight; she knows that Lucy could tell Mark.

But Lucy steps forward and hooks her arm inside Caz's arm, leaving Mark a pace behind. "If you want to know that," she says, "you'll just have to find your way there tonight, won't you?"

"You're mad," says Mark. "Both of you are barking mad."

It's just after midnight at the bandstand. A thin mist has peeled itself off the water and is prowling the riverbank. Mark has arrived, and Lucy and Caz have just told him what they do. The Creepy Thing.

"We don't take anything," Caz says.

"It's just a bit of fun," Lucy says.

"Fun!" Mark says. "Did you know people like to kill burglars if they catch them breaking into the house?"

"That's not true. Anyway, you have to steal stuff to be a burglar," Caz points out.

"Oh, so some bloke with a shotgun or an iron bar defending his house is going to know the difference! Excuse me, I don't think so! You've got a weird idea of fun." Mark sits down on the cold, concrete bandstand steps, arms folded, looking glum.

"So you're chickening out?" Lucy says.

"Thanks, but I'd rather have my dick tattooed by a chimpanzee. I can't believe I've come out at night for this."

"Afraid your mum will find out?" Lucy taunts. When

Mark turns away from her, she skips down the steps of the bandstand and makes her way across the grass towards the river's edge.

Caz sits next to Mark, but she keeps her eyes on Lucy, who is peering into the water. She doesn't want Lucy to accuse her of *making up*—Lucy's words—to Mark. "We don't hurt anyone. They don't even know we've been there. That's the point of it."

She can't find the words to explain to Mark why she does it. She wants to say that it's because of the *rush*. The tingle. The kind of excitement that makes your hair stand on end and your skin flush. The parachute moment. But she knows it will sound pathetic.

There is a reason why she does it. It's difficult to explain it away. Caz doesn't even like to think too much about it. Every time the thought of why she likes it crops up, she brushes it aside.

"It just seems sort of sad to me," Mark says, rescuing her from her own thoughts. "A sad thing to do."

She turns and looks into his eyes. There is a speck of moonlight swimming in his eyes, and Caz knows she'd rather be with him, even just sitting on these cold steps, than anything. But she's not going to *make up* to him. She's just not going to.

Lucy calls to them from the river's edge. "God! I turn my back for two minutes and here you are making up to him!"

"I am not!" Caz protests.

"Yes, you are."

"No, I'm not."

"Yes, you are! Did you snog while my back was turned?"

"Jesus!" Mark goes. "Jesus! You're like a pair of ten-year-olds!"

"You can talk, Mister Goody Two-shoes!" Caz says sharply. "I'll bet you're a virgin!"

"Are you?" Mark asks her.

She doesn't answer.

"Come on, let's go for a walk," Mark says.

"The three of us?"

"Just you and me."

"Can't."

"Why not?"

The truth is that Caz would like to go with him. Walk along the river in the mist. Maybe hold hands and kiss under the moonlight. There is nothing she would like better at that moment. She would like to know how his kiss might taste. But she won't, because Caz is loyal. "Lucy's my mate. You don't leave your mate."

Mark looks vexed. His brow wrinkles. He bares his teeth, and hugs himself briefly. "Cold," he says. "I'm going to split."

Caz watches him go. He walks away from the river, head down, towards the amber streetlamps.

Lucy appears beside her. "Wimp," she says. "Come on, let's do something."

CHAPTER FIVE
One Centimetre Away

"WHO LIVES HERE?" Caz whispers from in the bushes.

It's about half an hour since Mark went his own way. They've been prowling in the shadows, sizing up one or two targets. The house they have chosen, 13 Briar Street, is a small detached Victorian house with a badly neglected air. It is bounded by a hedge, so there is not much risk of them being seen by neighbours; not that many of them are still awake in the dead of night.

"A real skinny old bat. You must have seen her," Lucy says. "She's always in the supermarket buying a single can that she puts in one of those tartan shopping trolleys."

Caz does know, though she would rather she didn't. The old woman had once bumped into Caz outside the post office. "You wants to watch where youm a-goin', you do!" the old woman had said tartly. "You wants to be more careful of whom youm-a bangin' into, or you'll fetch summat home as you didn't expect!"

Caz had been too startled to answer on that day. All she remembered now was that the woman looked like the corpse of someone who had drowned at sea two hundred years ago and had come back to haunt the neighbourhood. Caz had asked her mother about the old woman. Helen had said her name was Mrs Tranter, and though she kept herself to herself, she was harmless.

Caz is dithering. For a moment she isn't sure about this game, especially after Mark dissed them for it. She keeps thinking about that word he used on her. *Sad.* But she's also annoyed. Cross with him for skipping away like that. Cross with Lucy. Cross with herself for not stopping him. When he left, the evening took a downward turn.

"You ready?" Lucy says.

Caz shrugs a yes for an answer, and they sneak up to the back window.

Lucy is becoming expert at this. She rocks the sash window. The wood is so rotten that she could practically lift the glass from its frame. She carries with her a thick metal ruler and all she has to do is insert the ruler between the upper and lower frames of the sash window until it butts against the fastening catch. Normally she would need to use a brick or a hammer to fetch the ruler a good, upright blow, but the catch floats open with a whisper at the merest touch from the ruler. Lucy raises an eyebrow at Caz. The silver light in her eye makes Caz think that Lucy looks like a tiny demon.

Lucy strips off her tracksuit top and places it against the pane of glass with the palms of both hands, easily pushing up the window. The curtains inside are drawn. Lucy slips her top back on and parts the curtains. The room inside seems to sigh with the admission of air damp from the mist and pearly from the moonlight. The girls climb in.

Inside the room is chilly.

"Colder in here than outside," Lucy whispers.

The room, softly lit by the moonlight streaming in at the window, is empty. Completely bare. There is not a stick of furniture. The walls are covered with ancient wallpaper of floral design, and there is a grim old carpet underfoot. Damp patches stain the walls. Again there is a smell: a mixture of damp and stale potpourri, and something unpleasantly sweet.

Here's where it kicks in for Caz. She already wants to get out. But that's the game: fighting against the screaming need to run. But you don't. You breathe through it, and you put one foot in front of the other and you keep going. You don't even know why.

Stepping across the room, they open the door. The door hinges whisper. They shuffle into the hall, each holding on to the other's arm, listening hard. A wall-mounted clock ticks loudly. After a moment they hear a car in the street outside. Its headlights wash the hallway as it passes by. The hall has a coatrack with two threadbare coats and a peculiar woollen hat hanging from it. There is a small table with an aspidistra plant in a white pot, and there in an old brass jar is the potpourri.

Caz breathes hard and looks at her friend. Lucy's eyes are weird in the weak, grey light. They are wide open. The pupils seem huge. Caz is still clutching Lucy's arm. Her fingers have been grabbing her sleeve so tightly she can't unclench them, but Lucy needs her to let go. Caz's white knuckles slowly unpick themselves from Lucy's sleeve. The urge to just run out—to stop this madness—takes over Caz again. She fights it off by counting backwards.

Lucy points upstairs. She goes first, clutching the banister rail and spreading her step, planting her feet at the very edge of the stairs so that they won't creak. Caz follows.

Lucy makes it to the top step before their luck gives out. The old banister creaks loudly. In the silence it sounds like wood splitting. The girls freeze and wait. There are things they know. They know that a mildly disturbed sleeper is more likely to roll over and go back to sleep than get out of bed. But knowing this doesn't make it easier. They wait for at least three minutes before making further progress up the stairs.

Three bedrooms present themselves, and all of the doors stand open. Lucy checks them out, quickly realising they have made a mistake. Lucy points down the stairs and whispers, "She's sleeping down there."

They make their descent of the stairs, trying to remember the creak points but the old varnished wood still cracks out a protest as they make their way back down. The front room downstairs has its door closed to them. As she stands in the hallway, inhaling the smell of potpourri, Caz's heart feels like it is dragging on her rib cage. Knocking and dragging. Her heart is like a bird that wants to get out of its cage, just as Caz wants to get out of the house. But she can't tear herself away, can't stop herself from doing this. Because the wind that's blowing through her right now—the wind in her hair as she hangs out of the aeroplane looking down into the darkness—makes her feel alive in every fibre of her body.

And it is just a game, isn't it? Not as if they actually hurt anyone. And the reason why Caz does it is because she can be half her age again. She can go back to a time when she could just be deliciously, recklessly badly behaved without having to pretend. A time before she had to take charge. A time before she had to be the one in control, with a mother who needs protecting; a time before her childhood was taken away and she suddenly had to be the responsible one. That's her favourite word right now: *irresponsible*. It's so wild to find a way to be *irresponsible*.

"Your turn," Lucy says.

Yes, it's Caz's turn. She takes a breath.

"Go on, then," Lucy whispers. "Get moving!"

Caz reaches out for the door handle and depresses it. The door is a little stiff but at last it swings open. Now they can hear the old woman breathing. It isn't a snore exactly, more a series of short sighs as the woman exhales in her sleep. It's dark in the room, but Caz can see that the old woman has her back to the door and is lying on her side. This makes things more difficult. It means that Caz is going to have to walk round to the other side of the bed to do the Creepy Thing.

And there is that smell again: the sickly sweet odour, like the smell flowers give off after they have been left to die in a vase. Thin, floating blades of streetlight are visible at the edges of the flower-patterned blue curtains. Caz feels Lucy's hand touch the small of her back, propelling her forward. She knows she has to take a step. She knows if she doesn't take that step forward in the next second that she will bottle it and run from the house and down the street, screaming into the night.

She walks quickly over to the other side of the bed, knowing this thing has to run for a count of fifteen seconds. Her stomach squeezes as she crouches beside the bed.

Fifteen seconds can be a very long time.

An alarm clock ticks loudly on the bedside table. It's an old-fashioned clock with a big face, roman numerals, and illuminated hands. Twin bells perch at the top of the clock with a hammer on either side poised to strike the bells. It's a minute before one o'clock in the morning.

Caz looks back at Lucy, who stands by the door. Lucy nods from the shadows. Caz bends over the sleeper, getting into position. She can smell the old woman's hair and skin.

She puts her nose just as close she can to the old woman's nose. A centimetre away. That's all there is to it. That's it. Except for the weird, weird count.

One.

The sleeper breathes out. Caz can actually feel the old woman's breath ripple across the pool of her own eye.

Two.

Time slows. Caz knows it does. She can feel time congeal, like water turning into ice.

Three.

She wants to look back, to see if Lucy is still there at the door, watching her. But she mustn't. She has to keep the count going.

Four.

The old woman smacks her lips lightly. Caz can see the deep lines of age on her face, and the crow's-feet around her eyes. The crow's-feet seem to twitch slightly in her sleep.

Five.

Time has frozen over now: it has become a solid block of ice, and now the block begins to stretch and expand, getting in the way of one second giving way to the next. Caz sees a picture of her mum sleeping inside the block of ice. Something happens so that the next counted number inside Caz's head seems itself to stretch and slow.

Siiiiiiiiiix.

Caz's heart is knocking and a feeling of cramp is spreading from her leg, but she remains perfectly still. The old woman breathes out again.

Sev–

A sudden whirr swells from the hall as the wall clock winds itself up for a single, loud chime. The chime sounds. It reverberates through the house like Big Ben and Caz holds her breath.

–ven

The rhythm of the old woman's breathing seems to have been changed by the chime from the clock. Her breath seems to catch in the back of her throat in a little piglike snort. It seems to Caz that the old woman has stopped breathing altogether. She looks hard at the face on the pillow. The woman's skin is peeling slightly. She has a light bloom of sweat on her brow.

Eight. Again Caz desperately wants to look up at Lucy, but she knows she mustn't. These are the rules of the Creepy Thing.

Niiiiiiiiiiiiiiiiine.

Caz's knows she's just a few seconds away.

Ten.

But in those few seconds she has a sudden and awful feeling that the old woman is dead. That by some horrible coincidence she has passed away, croaked it at the exact moment of Caz's Creepy.

Eleven.

Caz can't shake of the image of her mum encased in the block of ice. Then suddenly the image flashed inside her head, and it's not her mum in the ice, it's *her.*

Twelve.

Caz reaches out a hand just to try to touch back the sheet covering the old woman's mouth, just to lift it with the gentlest of movements, just to see if the woman really is dead.

Thirteen, and the old woman sits bolt upright in bed. She clamps her cold, steely hand over Caz's wrist.

Fourteen, and Caz screams and tries to pull away. There is a flutter at the door and the sound of Lucy bolting through the house, making her escape.

Fifteen, and Caz pulls away, but the old woman is incredibly strong. She grabs Caz's wrist with her other hand. Her touch is cold and metallic.

Shivering with fright, Caz looks down to see that the old woman has clamped onto her wrist a silver bracelet.

CHAPTER SIX

The Mark Behind the Shadow Behind the Bruise

AT THE END of the school day, Mark intercepts Lucy at the school gates. "Where's Caz?" he says. "Haven't seen her all day."

Lucy fingers the thin gold chain she wears around her neck. "Dunno." She puts the chain links in her mouth.

Perhaps it's the way that Lucy avoids looking him in the eye, but Mark senses something amiss. "Is she off sick?"

Lucy looks away again. With the gold chain links between her lips she grabs a hank of her long hair and pulls it tight behind her head, fixing it with a bobble. "Dunno."

From somewhere in the stream of schoolkids migrating from the school gates there comes a taunting cry. "Hey, Marky Marky! Izzat your girlfriend?"

He ignores it. "What time did you get home last night?"

Lucy is still fiddling with loose strands of her hair. She lets the chain drop from between her lips. "What do you care? You cleared off and left us soon enough!"

"Hey, Marky! Have you snogged her? Have you? Have you?"

"I only cleared off because—"

"Hey, Marky! Have you had a feel? Have you?"

"Wait," says Lucy.

She steps into the mass of school blazers and grabs the mouthing boy, a tall lad with a shock of blond hair, by his tie. She yanks him towards her. "Mark and I shag three times a day. We cover each other in liquid chocolate and lick each other's bodies from head to toe. We have great sex. We do all this while you play with yourself in your bedroom mirror, so what's your problem?"

She releases his tie and the lad steps back, red-faced. There are a few guffaws from his friends as they start pushing him around.

Lucy returns to Mark. "Wanker," she says.

"So," Mark says, "are you going to tell me what happened?"

Lucy gives Mark the bare bones of the evening, and then calls Caz. She stands by as the phone rings and rings. There is no answer. Lucy knows that Helen won't get home from work until almost six o'clock. But Caz, if she's in, should be picking up.

"I shouldn't have run off," Lucy says.

"Maybe not," says Mark.

"But that was our agreement. We said if one of us gets caught, the other should try to get away. We agreed there was no point both of us getting into trouble. We did agree that from the outset. We did."

"If you agreed that, well, that's it then, isn't it?"

"But I shouldn't have. You don't leave your best mate. You just don't."

"No."

"But we agreed."

Conrad shows up. "Why all the long faces?"

"C'mon," says Mark. "We'll go to the shop. Conrad will buy you a bag of nuts."

"You boys certainly know how to spoil a girl," says Lucy.

When Caz's mother gets back from her job at the Building Society, the telephone is ringing, but it stops just before she reaches it. The day's post is still strewn on the mat. Mostly it's junk mail. She hangs her keys on the hook by the front door and takes off her coat. Then she fills the kettle with water to make herself a cup of tea.

While the kettle is boiling she goes upstairs and into Caz's room. Her daughter is still sleeping. Helen puts her fingers to Caz's forehead, testing to see if she still has a fever. Caz does have a temperature, but it's light, and she doesn't wake. Helen wonders about calling for a doctor, then decides against it. She goes back downstairs and starts to prepare their evening meal.

The telephone rings again. It's Lucy, asking about Caz. She sounds worried. Helen reassures her that Caroline just has a fever, maybe a dose of the flu. No, Lucy can't speak to her because she's sleeping. Maybe when she wakes up Helen will get her to call. No, Helen doesn't think it's a good idea for Lucy to come round and visit. Why not? Because Caroline is tired and might still be sleeping. And anyway, Lucy wouldn't want to catch whatever it that Caroline has, now would she? That wouldn't make sense, now would it? Caroline will be back at school in a day or two, right as rain.

But Caroline—Caz—is not right as rain.

In fact it's raining in her dream. The rain is coming down so hard she can't get home. The streets are flooding, becoming a river, and the silver bracelet on her wrist is so heavy she can't lift her arm out of the water that is rising fast. There are police frogmen swimming under the water, looking for old people swept away by the torrent. The old people swim up to Caz and grab the bracelet. They are still pulling at the bracelet, trying to get it off her wrist when she surfaces.

She wakes up, desperately needing to pee. Her hand flies to her wrist, where the bracelet was, and it has gone. She doesn't know whether to feel relieved or upset by losing it. Her wrist is sore. There is a livid red mark where the silver rubbed against her. She gets out of bed and goes to the toilet.

"You're awake," Helen says, standing at the top of the stairs as Caz comes out of the bathroom.

Caz's hand flies to her wrist again, now concealing the livid marks left behind by the bracelet.

"Do you feel better? I've made you something to eat. Do you want to come downstairs? Lucy called for you."

"I'll be down," says Caz.

Caz doesn't have much of an appetite. Fact is, Caz has been puking. It is something that started just after she got away from the old woman's house.

The old woman had woken and clamped the bracelet onto Caz's wrist like a handcuff. The hag had been smiling a sick, hideous grin that bared the yellow pegs of her teeth. Her old eyes were shining, too, filled with milky moonlight. She hadn't said anything, just sprang up in bed, smiled with that twisted mouth of hers, and clamped the bracelet on Caz's wrist.

Lucy was already gone before Caz had worked out what had happened. Caz had jerked her arm back but the old woman's grip had been strong. She seemed to trace the pattern on the bracelet with a bony old finger and then, suddenly, let Caz go before lying back on her bed with a deep sigh.

Released, Caz had made a run for it. She'd charged out of the bedroom and had almost flung herself along the hallway corridor to get away. Forgetting that they'd got into the house by the rear window, instead she'd hurled herself at the door, scrabbling at the bolts barring her escape. There had been three bolts on the door. All the time her fingernails were breaking against the metal bolts she was sure the old woman was behind her, about to grab her again.

But she'd got out. She'd run down the street until her lungs simply seized. She'd stood in a bus shelter, trying to breathe, not laughing this time but trying to open the catch on the bracelet to get it off her wrist, all the while looking back down the street to see if the old woman was after her. When her breath came back and her heart began to still, she vomited behind the bus shelter.

She'd continued to retch on her way home, but something bothered her far more than this sickness. The bracelet: she couldn't get it off. No matter how much she fiddled with the clasp, she couldn't seem to find a catch, a lever, a way to break the thing open. It didn't hurt or feel especially heavy, though it did feel a little icy on her skin. But no matter how much she struggled with the thing, it resisted all her efforts to break it open.

When she eventually reached home, she immediately went to the kitchen drawer. Finding a blunt knife, she tried to slide the blade into the joint of the bracelet. It was useless. She found a corkscrew and tried to use its point to twist and prise the thing open, but to no avail. Caz raked through the kitchen drawer, dragging at knives, meat skewers, egg whisks, and a dozen useless implements. Then she had to race to the bathroom to puke again.

After that she rinsed her mouth and dabbed cold water on her face. She examined her face in the mirror. She looked awful. Her skin was white like a death mask, and sweat had plastered her hair to her head. The pupils of her eyes had shrunk to tadpoles swimming in a gluey pond. As she lifted her hand to her hair, the bracelet gleamed in the mirror, slightly blue.

The bracelet itself was quite ordinary: a thick, silver band engraved with a faint pattern. The pattern, when examined, was like the scales on the long curving tail of perhaps a snake or a lizard, but whatever it was, it had no head. Perhaps it wasn't a tail, maybe it was a tongue. Whatever the thing was, Caz just wanted to get it off her wrist. It felt like a prisoner's manacle.

Exhausted, Caz had gone back to the kitchen. In another drawer she found a pair of pliers and had taken them to bed with her. Still fiddling uselessly with the pliers, and failing to make any impression on the bracelet, she'd fallen asleep.

And now that she's awake, and the bracelet has gone, her mother has made something for her to eat, even though she knows she won't be able to keep anything down. She feels dazed and scared by her ordeal, and sick as a dog. But her first concern is to go back and find the bracelet, which must have worked its way off her wrist in the night.

Back in her bedroom she finds the pair of pliers under her pillow. She strips the bed and flings her pillow across the room, but there is no sign of the sinister piece of jewellery. She gets down on her hands and knees and looks under the bed. She looks everywhere: on her desk, on the chest of drawers, and the windowsill. It simply can't be.

She can understand that it might have worked its way free in the night, but it should be there. It should be right there! Right there!

"What are you looking for?"

It's Helen. She's got her head round the bedroom door.

"My book." Caz says. "I've lost my book."

"Your dinner is getting cold. Fish pie. Your favourite."

Caz gets to her feet and runs to the bathroom.

That fish pie isn't sitting too well at all. In fact Caz, lying on the sofa watching junk TV, feels herself like a dead fish in a polluted lake. Her mother is on the phone to her mysterious boyfriend. Helen is giving him that high, tinkly laugh, the antidepressant laugh she uses when she's pretending to be jolly, and she's pretending to be jolly now. The fog of the pills put a stop to any real, deep-in-the-gut laughs years ago. "Oh, that's so funny! Tee-hee!" She actually almost speaks the words *tee-hee-hee*. Why laugh when you don't feel it? is what Caz thinks.

Helen puts down the phone. "Well. I've arranged to see him again tomorrow evening. That's assuming you're recovering."

"Tee-hee-hee," says Caz.

"Oh, don't be such a little witch," Helen says, stung. "At least when you're being mean I can see that you're getting better."

I'm not, Caz thinks, *I'm really not.*

She's worried about her wrist. Caz has spent the entire

evening trying to make sure that Helen can't see what's happening to her skin. The livid red mark where the bracelet was has now died down, but it has left behind it a blue-black shadow. Almost like a bruise.

But it's not a bruise exactly. It doesn't hurt at all. It's not like a scratch or a bump or any kind of abrasion from the bracelet.

Caz thinks it's starting to look like a tattoo.

CHAPTER SEVEN

He's Looking at Your Legs

"I WANT TO ask you about something," Helen says to Caz over breakfast the next morning.

Caz doesn't like the casual tone of her mother's voice. She's trying to sound too relaxed. As if whatever is on her mind isn't important. It's the way she's saying it, as if she's just remembered it. It's like her mother is *acting* as though she's just remembered it. Caz pulls her sleeve a little farther down over the peculiar tattoo on her wrist. "What's that then?" Caz mutters through a mouthful of breakfast cereal.

"When I came down yesterday morning. You were still in bed. There was all this stuff on the kitchen worktop."

"Stuff? What stuff?"

"Oh, I cleaned it all away. It was stuff from the kitchen

drawer. Knives. Bottle openers. Corkscrews. Tin openers. Skewers. Like everything had been dumped out of the kitchen drawer."

Caz flashes back on the moment she'd desperately tried to hack away at the bracelet on her arm. She must have gone to bed and left all the kitchen implements where they were. "Oh, yes. I came down in the night. I was looking for something."

There is a silence as Helen swallows her cornflakes. "What? What were you looking for?"

Caz says, "I can't even remember. You know what? I think I was sleepwalking. And then I woke up."

"Sleepwalking?"

"I think so."

"That doesn't sound good."

"No."

"There's another thing. The door was open."

"What?" Caz drops her spoon in her dish.

"Just ajar, a little. But open. Like anybody could have walked in here while we were sleeping."

"Gosh."

"You hadn't been out, had you? I mean, you don't go out while I'm fast asleep, do you? I know it would take a bomb to wake me . . ."

"No!" Caz lies. "I mean, maybe I opened it while I was sleepwalking. Though I wouldn't know, would I?"

Helen pushes back her chair and gets up. She's ready to go to work. "Oh, well, if you say it was sleepwalking, that's good enough for me."

Caz hears Helen sweep upstairs and come back down again as she readies to leave for work. But something is still bothering Caz: the fact that she knows her mother doesn't believe her for a single second. Caz was lying and her mother knows it. That in itself doesn't bother Caz unduly. What disturbs her is that she seems to have the ability this morning to see behind everything her mother says. It is as if, this morning only, she can see into her mother's heart.

It's not easy to say why. If spoken words were written on a page in ordinary black ink, it would be as if the lies, the slight deceptions, were written in blue ink and capital letters.

Helen pops her head round the door. "Have a good day at school. You haven't forgotten I'm going out this evening, have you?"

The mysterious boyfriend. No, Caz hasn't forgotten. "Oh, yeah. Out with . . . what did you say his name was?"

Helen smiles sweetly. "I didn't say. Bye!"

After the door slams behind Helen, Caz inches her sleeve up her wrist to look again at the creepy tattoo.

It's glowing.

At school that morning, Caz has to wait until first break before she can speak to Lucy about everything that has happened. That means sitting through Maths, trying to concentrate on algebra while trying to decide if the tattoo on her wrist is tingling or if she is only imagining it is tingling. Every few minutes she can't resist sliding back her sleeve and inspecting the tattoo under the cover of her desk.

There is no doubt in Caz's mind that the tattoo is indeed glowing. Faintly only, but shining with a dull silver light. The tattoo itself is a replication of the shape of the bracelet—a simple blue-green band around her wrist. But inside the band is some sort of design. It's impossible to say whether the design is any more than a simple wavy line, or whether it is a snake or serpent: perhaps one that eats its own tail. It's just too faint to make out clearly, and the closer she peers at it the more it seems to take on the natural colours of Caz's own skin. In direct sunlight she can barely see it at all, but in shadow the design shows up much more clearly. And when Caz holds her wrist on her lap under the cover of her desk, well then there is no mistake: it shines, dull, but with its own remarkable light.

It scares her. It makes Caz feel ill all over again.

She's shaken out of her thoughts when a voice whispers in her ear. "Know what? He fancies you!"

This is Sally, who sits next to her in Maths. Sally is exceptionally tall. She also has unnaturally large breasts for her age. She comes to school in fishnet tights and often tries to get away with wearing lipstick. Sally has a rep for going out with boys five or six years older than herself.

"What?"

"I've been watching him. He can't take his eyes off you."

Sally nods towards the front of the class and Caz realises Sally is talking about Mr Corkhill, who has his back turned and who is busy scribbling algebraic equations on the board. "Rubbish!"

"I'm serious," Sally whispers. "He keeps staring at you. He's been looking at your legs."

Caz takes a swipe at Sally. The thought of Mr Corkhill—*Corky*—looking at her legs does not excite her. True, one or two of the teachers at Dovelands are fanciable: Mr Simms the English teacher, and—at a pinch—Mr Williams, who teaches French. But Corkhill? Ugh! No. Absolutely not. Quite apart from the fact that Corky has pasty skin and the eyes of a dead shark, he parts his hair in the middle and . . . no, no, no. "He's more your type," Caz tells Sally.

Sally takes a swipe back at Caz, just before Mr Corkhill turns from the board and back to the class. Now Caz can't resist looking up to see if he is looking at her. And it's true. He *does* seem to be regarding her rather strangely.

Caz responds by keeping her head well down until the end of the lesson. But when the bell goes, Mr Corkhill outlines their homework and says, "Caroline, could you see me after the others have gone, please?"

Sally gathers up her books and jiggles her eyebrows at Caz. But Caz can't say anything because Mr Corkhill at the front of the class has his arms folded and is waiting for the others to leave.

"Good luck," Sally whispers before leaving.

When all of Caz's classmates have gone, Corkhill steps across the silent classroom. Still with his arms folded, he plants himself squarely before Caz. She doesn't like the expression on his face. It is part-disapproving, part-smirking. He waits, staring at her. Caz blinks at him.

"Were you in a hurry to get out of my lesson, Caroline?" Mr Corkhill says.

Caz shrugs. "Not especially."

"Not especially? Well, it seemed to me that every few minutes you couldn't resist taking a peek at your wristwatch. As if you couldn't wait for the lesson to pass!"

So that was it. Caz wants to explain that she wasn't wearing a wristwatch. But she thinks better of it. "Sorry."

"I'm a little disappointed. You didn't seem terribly interested in the lesson today."

Caz shrugs again. Mr Corkhill stares down at her, with that dangerous smirk on his face.

At last he says, "All right. Off you go."

Caz gets up to leave. She can feel his eyes boring into her back. It can't be true, she thinks as she leaves the classroom. Surely Sally can't be right. It can't be that Corky has the hots for her, can it? Ugh!

Caz shakes her head, trying to put the horrible thought aside. Then she goes off in search of Lucy.

It's in the girls' toilet at break time. Caz makes Lucy wait until the place is clear, then drags Lucy into one of the cubicles. Not until she's slammed the door and shot home the bolt does she show Lucy the tattoo.

"That's weird," is all Lucy can say. "Weird."

"Sometimes it glows," Caz says. "It isn't glowing now, but I swear to you that sometimes it glows."

Lucy sniggers. But it isn't a snigger of merriment, it's a

snigger of fear. She knows her friend isn't messing around. "Have you tried to wash it off?"

"What the hell do you think? I've tried scrubbing my skin raw. It won't come off."

"What happened to the bracelet?"

"I've no idea. It must have fallen off, and now I can't find it. I've turned the house upside down looking for it."

"This is just so weird!"

"Stop saying that, will you!" Caz is cross with Lucy. "Don't—" But someone comes into the toilet. Lucy puts a finger to her lips and they fall silent as they hear someone enter one of the other cubicles.

Caz suddenly feels very small. After going around acting so grown-up and reckless and treating everything as a joke, she feels scared: deep-down scared. Something has happened to her and she doesn't know what it is. She only knows that she has been marked out. Hot angry tears well up in her eyes. It's the first time she's cried since it happened and now she can't stop it coming. She wipes her eyes, then Lucy surprises her by hugging her close.

"We'll sort it," Lucy whispers. "Don't worry."

"How?" Caz mouths at her, desperate for a solution. "How will we?"

"I don't know. But I'll come up with something."

CHAPTER EIGHT:
There's a Mirror on the Ceiling

"YOU GO IN FIRST," Caz says, trying to steer Lucy ahead of her.

"I don't think so!" Lucy says.

"But it was your idea!"

"Yes, my idea, but your tattoo! This is for you, don't forget."

Caz tries to peer inside the tattoo parlour, but the windows are all blanked out. The glass is either painted over or blocked by design samples. The tattoo parlour is in a run-down part of town: the neighbouring shops include a dodgy sex store and a newsagent with all its windows protected by wire mesh. Caz glances up and down the street. A lone scrap of filthy newspaper is chased along the gutter by a light wind.

"Come on!" Lucy urges. "Just open the door!"

Yes, Lucy's idea, but Caz has seen this place before. It has a handwritten sign in the window: WE NOW ALSO DO TATTOO REMOVALS. Lucy's proposal is just to go in to get some advice. But there is another sign, bigger, bolder, printed. It reads: IF YOU'RE UNDER 18 YOU CAN SOD OFF.

"Oh, for God's sake!" Lucy pushes open the door.

Heavy rock music is playing, but at low volume, from a beat-up tape machine in the corner of the shop. Sitting in a beat-up executive chair and reading a newspaper is a giant. He wears a clean white T-shirt and his huge pink gut spills over the massive silver buckle securing his black jeans. His long hair is tied in a neat ponytail, and he has a forked beard like a wizard out of a bad fairy tale. The beard is dyed purple. He looks like a grizzled biker. Though if he is the tattooist, he bears none of the tattooist's art anywhere on his arms, nor on the visible expanse of pink gut.

He doesn't bother to look at them. He merely sniffs and turns a page of the newspaper. Then he says, in a low murmur that sounds like his voice box has been burned out by a million cigarettes, "You two can sod off."

"What?" Lucy shouts.

"You're not eighteen. Neither of you. So sod off."

"You haven't even looked at us!" Lucy protests, boldly.

The tattooist floats a stubby, nicotine-stained finger into the air and points at the ceiling. The girls look up. There is a giant mirror screwed to the ceiling, through which he must have looked at them when they walked in. He drops his hand and turns over a page of the newspaper. "Still here?" he croaks.

"We want to ask you something," Lucy says, growing in confidence. Caz is amazed at Lucy. Her own instinct is to run out of the door.

"The answer is no, unless certain conditions apply, and under those circumstances the answer is still no."

"Aren't you the funny one in the family!" Lucy shoots back.

The biker-tattooist drops his newspaper to his lap and looks at them directly for the first time. His face is tanned. His skin looks like the leather on an old-fashioned school satchel. He blinks at them. Then the skin around his eyes crinkles. "Well," he says, "we've got a live one here. Do you realise I could probably get arrested for just letting you walk into my shop?"

"I don't believe it," Lucy replies, "and anyway we're not here to get a tattoo. We want to know about getting one removed. Surely you don't have to be eighteen to get one removed!"

The tattooist strokes his beard. "No. That's a horse of a different colour. Show me."

"It's not me," Lucy says, stepping aside for Caz. "It's her."

His gaze switches to Caz. When he speaks you can almost hear the tobacco tar dripping in his throat. "Can she speak for herself? Let's have a look. Come on then—it's not on yer butt, is it?"

"No," Caz says. She steps across to the man and rolls back her sleeve.

Before he looks at her, the tattooist reaches for a pair of tortoiseshell round-rimmed spectacles. Suddenly he looks more like an eccentric professor than a biker. He takes Caz's arm, and his touch is surprisingly gentle. He turns her wrist so that he can examine the tattoo back and front. "Who gave you this?"

Caz hesitates. Lucy jumps in for her. "Her boyfriend did it. But she wants it taken off."

"Don't bullshit me," the tattooist says gently, "or I won't help you. Unless your boyfriend is a master tattooist he didn't do this. It's all perfectly even. Faint. But even. Incredibly good work. Too good, really. I've not seen one like it."

"Can you get rid of it?" Caz asks him.

The tattooist sucks in his breath. "Complicated. Fizz, just take a look at that work!"

Caz is shocked when a tiny woman gets up from a chair in the corner of the shop. She's wearing all black, and sunglasses, even though it's so gloomy inside. It's spooky: the girls have been in the shop fully five minutes and Caz never even noticed the woman in that time. In fact she seems to take shape from some black curtains hanging against the wall.

The woman he called Fizz takes her sunglasses off and looks at Caz's arm. Then she shapes her mouth into a pout and makes her lips pop, and shrugs, before going back to her seat in the corner.

"Is it my imagination, or is it glowing?" the tattooist asks.

Caz doesn't answer. She is still staring at the almost-invisible woman while the tattooist explains a few facts about removing tattoos. Red, black, and blue ink are the easiest to remove, he says. Green and yellow are the hardest. Caz's tattoo is blue-green, almost turquoise, and that makes it more difficult. "You can cut 'em out, freeze 'em out, or rub them out. All very painful. Or you can burn 'em out with lasers, which is what I do. Supposed to be painless, but I'd be a liar if I said it was totally pain-free." He points to his qualifications in the form of a framed certificate hanging on the wall. "Fifty-five pounds a session."

"Fifty-five quid!" Caz exclaims. "Where the hell am I going to get fifty-five quid!"

The woman in the corner shakes her head.

"That's just for starters," says the tattooist. "You're going to need anything between five and ten sessions."

"Not cheap, is it?" Lucy exclaims.

"Listen babe, we put 'em on and we take 'em off. These days we get half of our business from people wanting 'em taken off. You're lucky your tattoo doesn't say *I shagged Toby*. Why not leave it just as it is?"

"Huh," says Caz, looking at the tattooist's undecorated arms. She also notices that the woman has none, either. "How come you don't have tattoos?"

"Do I look dumb?" The tattooist cackles. Then he slumps back in his seat and picks up his newspaper. "Let me know if you get the cash together."

Caz pushes Lucy towards the door, but before leaving Lucy can't resist asking him, "What are the mirrors on the ceiling for?"

Caz looks up at the mirror. She can see herself, Lucy, and the tattooist in the chair with his newspaper. But she can't see the woman he called Fizz. Yet when she looks back, the woman is still there, staring at Caz strangely from behind her sunglasses. Caz looks at the mirror again. It doesn't add up.

"I'd tell you," the tattooist says without even looking up from his newspaper, "but you're not eighteen."

"Come on," says Lucy.

She almost has to drag Caz from the shop.

Hiding the tattoo from Helen is easy enough for Caz. Hiding her mood isn't quite so easy. Helen is getting ready to go out with Mister Mystery, as Caz has taken to calling her mother's new boyfriend. She's laying on the makeup a bit thick, Caz thinks. Helen has gone in for pink lippy, too, applying it in the bedroom mirror while Caz wonders about her mother and what or who she is getting into. Sometimes the fog-pills make her mum a little too relaxed about things. The roles are reversed: she wants to give her mum advice about dating boys: *Be yourself. Don't try too hard. Don't seem too keen. Don't drink too much or he'll think you're a pushover.*

"Are you all right, Caroline?" Helen says, popping her pink lips at the mirror. "Only you look so *worried* these days. Do you think this pink lipstick is a bit too much?"

"It's fine."

"It's not me you're worried about, is it? Not worried

about me going out with this bloke? It's only a bit of fun, you know, nothing serious. I'd tell you if it got serious."

There it is again, that itch: somehow Caz knows that her mother *does* have serious notions about this man. "It's not that, Mum."

Helen can't seem to fix her earring. "What is it then, bab? Something's worrying you."

"I've told you not to call me bab. It sounds stupid."

"Can you fix this for me?"

Caz fixes the clasp on her mother's earring. When it's done, she steps back. "There. Let's look at you. Not bad. Have you got a condom?"

Helen makes as if to whack her daughter round the ear. Even though Helen would never hit her, Caz ducks anyway.

A car horn sounds outside. Caz races across the room to take a look, ignoring her mother's protests to come away from the window. It's no use anyway. She can't make out the driver.

"Why doesn't he ever get out of the car and come to the door?" Caz says.

Helen is already halfway down the stairs. "I've told you, he's shy," she says over her shoulder. "I won't be late, but don't wait up if you want to go to bed."

"One thing," Caz shouts downstairs before her mother closes the door. "Take the chewing gum out of your mouth before you snog him."

Helen turns to give her an old-fashioned look before closing the door behind her, leaving Caz in the silence of the house.

The first thing Caz does is check her tattoo. It seems to have stopped glowing. Caz has noticed that the curious, dull, luminous shine comes and goes. She doesn't know why. But the fact that that the tattoo does behave in this way makes her want to keep checking it, something she can't easily do when Helen is around. Because if Helen discovers that she has a tattoo, Helen will go *apeshit.*

But what Caz does need to think about, after she has finished inspecting her own wrist tattoo, is money. The laser treatment is astronomically expensive. At the minimum she is going to have to find two hundred and fifty pounds. Caz has no idea where she's going to get that kind of money.

Helen has always encouraged her to keep a savings account at the Building Society, where she works. She has a savings book that she keeps in her sock drawer. Caz rummages through her socks to find the book. She's nervous about sock drawers. One time, a couple of years back, she came home from school to find her mother crying her eyes out over a sock drawer.

"Too many odd ones," was all she could get out of her weeping, bawling mother, "too many odd socks." At least the pills seemed to make the odd socks go away. Caz digs through the pop socks and sports socks and knotted nylons and finds her savings book.

She sits on her bed to look at it, even though she already knows how much is in there, because she draws from it often. Fifteen pounds and twelve pence. She lets the Building Society book fall from her hands to the bed.

Helen keeps household money in a battered old tea caddy on the kitchen shelf. Caz is allowed to dip into it for grocery shopping, or to pay the milkman. Helen trusts her, and Caz has repaid that trust by never taking anything without asking first. Money is very tight in their household. Caz has always been given cash for the things she needs, and she's clever enough to know the difference between needs and wants.

Caz pads downstairs and lifts the tea caddy from the shelf. She counts out the money. In folded twenty-pound notes there is one hundred and twenty pounds, plus some loose change.

Caz puts the money back and returns the tea caddy to the shelf. She's not about to steal from her own mother. In her mind that would mark her out as the lowest of the low.

No, there has to be another way.

If she takes a job, maybe at the weekends, or delivering junk newspapers in the evening, perhaps she could raise the money. But it would take months to make anywhere near enough. The point of the laser treatment is to get rid of the tattoo quickly, firstly so that Caz's mother won't spot it, and secondly (and more crucially) so that she won't have to explain how she came to have it.

How she came to have it.

The very thought puts a huge lead ball in Caz's stomach. She doesn't want to think about it. She switches on the television and watches it for half an hour. Then she completes some homework. Halfway through the evening Lucy calls her to ask if she'd thought any more about the money. Caz tells her she hasn't stopped thinking about it.

At around ten o'clock Caz, slumped on the sofa, hears a car draw up outside.

Helen comes in quickly. "Is it tidy?" she says nervously. She starts plumping up cushions and carrying out some shoes Caz has left lying around.

"Why?" says Caz, sitting up.

Helen switches off the TV set. "He's coming in," she whispers. "For a nightcap."

Caz is wide-eyed. Mister Mystery is about to show his face. "Does the TV have to go off?"

"He doesn't like TV. Oh, here he is." Helen rushes back to the front door to let the man in.

Helen leads the man into the living room. Caz just can't stop her jaw from dropping. She blinks at him.

"Well," Helen says, suddenly very formal. "I believe you two might have already met."

"Good evening, Caroline," says Mr Corkhill. "I hope you've done your maths homework!"

CHAPTER NINE

Really Not That Bad

CAZ IS LEFT with a painful wide-mouth grin on her face for the next half an hour. Yes, she agrees, it is a surprise. No, she concedes, she never expected it, not for a minute. Yes, she admits, she thought he was looking at her a bit strangely in Maths today. And the grin on her face, even though it's making her cheeks ache, even though she hates the fact that it's plastered to her mouth—just won't go away!

Until after half an hour, when he excuses himself to go to the bathroom, that is. Caz is livid.

"What do you think?" Helen says before Caz has a chance to speak.

"What do I think? What do I think? I think you must be barking mad!"

Helen is shocked. This is not the reaction she expected.

"Well, I thought you'd be a bit surprised, but he's not that bad, Caroline!"

"Not that bad! He's a geek! I can't believe you would do this to me! My own mother is not just going out with one of my teachers, if that wasn't enough to get me crucified at school! No! She has go out with Mister Pond Life, the most hideous biological specimen in the staffroom! I'll be slaughtered! I'll be torn apart! I'll be—"

The upstairs toilet cistern flushes. "Pull yourself together," Helen hisses. "And don't let him hear you say words like 'crucified.'"

"What?"

Mr Corkhill reappears, beaming. Caz can't understand it, but her painful smile reappears on her lips, too. She can't seem to stop it, even though she feels like shredding the sofa cushions with her teeth.

"I should get going," he says.

"Oh," Helen simpers, "you don't have to rush off yet."

"Don't want to be too late. We've both got school tomorrow, haven't we, Caroline? Wouldn't want the pupils to hear I'd been out until the small hours!"

What on earth is he talking about? thinks Caroline. For one thing it's only ten thirty; for another thing, does he actually think that I'm going to broadcast to everyone at school that he's been at my house making out with my mum? Does he think I'm going to publish a school newspaper about the whole catastrophe?

"I'll see you to the car," Helen says.

"Good night then, Caroline," Corkhill says.

"Good night, Mr Corkhill."

"Oh, you'd better start calling me Neville if we're going to be seeing more of each other. Not at school, though. Better to remain formal in class!"

Caz nods. He's right. They'd better remain formal at school. Otherwise she might just feel like hurling herself under the school bus. Or leaping headfirst from the school roof. Or hanging herself from the netball post.

After he's gone, Helen comes back in and says, "Come on, Caroline, he's really not that bad."

"Not that bad? That really is the bottom of the barrel. I mean, after you've scraped away at whatever stuff is rotting at the bottom of the barrel, that is."

"No, you're being cruel," Helen said, "and you'd better button it, 'cos I won't put up with cruelty."

"But why him, Mum? Of all the blokes you might bring back here?"

"Look, I find him attractive, even if you don't."

It's right there that Caroline gets a tiny jolt, a little fizz of electricity. It's that something she's been feeling for the last couple of days, but this time it's strong. It's a tiny warning in her brain, and it tells her this: *Her mum is lying.*

Lying. Why would she lie? Why say she likes him when she doesn't?

"It's not true. You don't fancy him at all. You're even lying to yourself."

At first Helen looks angry at this. Then she looks exhausted. In the next moment her eyes fill with tears. She collapses on the sofa and weeps fully.

Oh, I am such a shit, thinks Caz. "I'm sorry, Mum. I didn't mean to upset you. It was just such a shock. Him being my teacher and everything. Here, let me get you a tissue."

Helen sits up and blows her nose. "You don't understand how hard it is for me, Caroline. You're right, Neville isn't my first choice for a partner, but I'm not eighteen. I'm too shy to go out to a pub or to a club to find someone. Anyway, I don't want someone for a one-night stand. It's no fun and it's too upsetting. I want someone who will care, for both of us. And he's kind, Caroline. He's kind to me. No, he might not look like a glamour model, but there's more to a decent person than stunning good looks."

Caz can't really see that. But what she can see is another round of tears coming. "Come with me," she says. "I'll make you a cup of tea."

Helen obediently follows Caz into the kitchen. "He's all right when you get to know him. You'll see."

"I'm sure you're right," Caz says, biting her lip. "It's not so bad. Just so long as we can keep quiet about it at school."

And they both laugh. Sort of. Heck, thinks Caz, I'm developing an antidepressant laugh myself. It's catching.

Now Caz has two monstrous things to hide. Her bracelet-tattoo and her mum's boyfriend. It's difficult for her to decide which one is the most scary. If she had a laser torch, she would burn the first one from her wrist, and the thought of the second one from her brain. But she has this instinct, this deep feeling, that one thing has triggered the other.

Bad luck.

Caz is sure that the tattoo is a curse that brings with it bad luck. The kind of bad luck that would start bringing freaky people into your life. She starts to think about other things that may have gone wrong in her life lately.

Fortunately, she doesn't have Maths the next day at school, so she doesn't have to face "Neville" Corkhill.

At lunchtime, she's standing in the playground near the cycle sheds and Lucy walks up to her with her big idea. Lucy has been thinking about how Caz can earn some money. "The Black Dog," says Lucy, gazing at Caz fiercely. Lucy has a nasty purple-and-yellow bruise on her arm. Caz knows where it came from. She also knows enough not to ask about it. It's just *too* personal. In movies and TV dramas everyone says: *Let's talk about it*. In real life no one ever has to say: *Let's* not *talk about it*.

"What?"

"The Black Dog," repeats Lucy, as if that explains everything. "They're looking for casual staff, especially at weekends. Four pounds an hour. Two weekends would about pay for one laser session."

The Black Dog is a vinegary old boozer's pub on the hill by the castle. It has a reputation for being rough. As in *dog-rough*.

"Aren't you forgetting one thing? We're not old enough. You can't work behind a bar until you're eighteen."

"Not *serving*," Lucy says, as if she's talking to a small child, "but *collecting* the *glasses*. And we're both old enough for that."

"And you can't work after seven o'clock until you're

sixteen." Caz knows all this stuff. She's considered various jobs to try to boost the household budget.

Lucy is less impressed by the legal obstacles. "We could work together. I'll give you my wages towards the treatment."

Caz looks at her friend. Whatever anyone thinks about Lucy, she is incredibly loyal. The other strange thing is that Caz knows for certain that she's not lying when she says she'll hand over her wages. It's that itch again. "Do you mean that?" Caz says. "You'd give me what they'd pay you?"

Lucy's big brown eyes don't even blink. "Well, some of it," she says lightly.

Caz doesn't know what to say, but she's saved from speaking.

"What you two talking about? Looks serious." It's Mark.

"We've both got a job," Lucy brags. "Collecting glasses at The Black Dog."

Mark sucks air between his teeth. "Black Dog? Dirty Dog, more like."

"Is it?" asks Caz.

"The police tried to close it down 'cos of all the fighting and—"

"Not that bad!" Lucy protests

"—they busted all these crackheads who were using the place to score their dope and—"

"Wrong place," says Lucy.

"—my brother stopped going in 'cos he said that you

needed Wellington boots to paddle through all the spilled beer and blood and—"

"Stop going on!" Lucy shouts.

"—if you don't believe me ask Julie Waddell—she stopped working there 'cos some drunk woman put a hand up her skirt and—"

"Woman?"

"Yeah, and that was after she'd had her handbag stolen on the same night."

Lucy's had enough. She grabs Mark by the tie and pushes him up against the cycle-shed wall. "Shut up, will you! I've just got her a job there!"

Mark laughs, holding up his hands as a peace offering.

"Somehow," says Caz, "I'm going right off the idea."

"Oh," says Lucy. "Please yourself. If you don't want to . . ." But she trails off and just stares at Caz with her eyes popping.

"Don't want to what?" Mark wants to know.

"Oh, forget it!" Lucy spits, and she storms across the playground in search of less stupid company.

"Wow! She's a packet of fireworks, inn't she?" Mark says. "Wanna come to the cinema with me one night?"

CHAPTER TEN
That's a Bad Shirt

THEY DO GO to the cinema one evening. Mark has a friend at the box office who, he says, will let them into an 18-rated movie. They snog a little outside the cinema, then they go in.

Mark pays for the pair of them. It's not that Caz wants to take his money: she's the kind of girl who likes to pay her way. But Mark had already brushed aside her shortage of cash as no reason for them not to go.

They watch *Red Juice,* which is a seriously bad horror movie. It's the usual stuff: kids trying to have sex all get the chop from a masked psycho with a gleaming meat hatchet. Mark puts his arm around her shoulders almost as soon as they sit down. She lets him. Just when the screen is most like an abattoir, with teenage limbs floating in a river of blood and gore and white walls splattered with red puddles, Mark thinks this is a good time to reach over and cup his hand round her breast.

Funny timing, Caz thinks, but she doesn't stop him.

At a dragging point during the movie Caz looks along the row of seats. There aren't too many people in the cinema for this evening's screening of *Red Juice.* But there, on the end of the row and just one tier in front, is someone she thinks she knows. It's a small woman with a head of curly black hair. Bizarrely, in the darkness of the cinema, she's wearing sunglasses.

Caz tries to remember her name. Fizz, that's it: the woman from the tattoo parlour. It seems Fizz senses that she's being stared at, for she looks over her shoulder and down the line of seats at Caz. She pops her lips briefly at Caz before returning her attention to the big screen.

Mark doesn't chance his arm any farther than his little breast squeeze. Though at a certain point in the movie, he does lift her hand to his mouth to kiss her fingers. She turns from the screaming, freaking, blue-funk mayhem on screen to smile at him. Their eyes flash on each other like torches in the dark of the cinema. He kisses her fingers again, and she thinks, *Well, yeah, he* is *pretty good-looking.* Then Mark goes to kiss her wrist but he sees something shining there, shining out of the blackness.

He pulls up short. "What's that?" he whispers.

Caz pulls away from his hand and draws her sleeve back across the tattoo. "Nothing."

They both return their stares to the screen. The psycho

with the shiny meat hatchet is revealed as the school-teacher—*Oh, my God, it's almost Neville Corkhill!*—but for Caz the movie has already died along with most of its cast. She's wondering if he'll bring up the matter of the tattoo later.

He does, when he walks her home.

"Let me look at that thing on your wrist," Mark says as they approach her house.

"What thing?" Caz is just playing for time. *One hundred yards to go,* she thinks, *and I was sure I'd get away without him mentioning it.*

"That tattoo thing on your wrist. Let me see it."

"It's not a tattoo."

"Oh? What is it?"

"It's just kids' stuff. Silly. I'll wash it off as soon as I get in."

But he insists. He steps in front of her and stops her from moving forward. "Go on!" he laughs. "Let me see!"

She nips round him and walks more quickly towards her house. Mark thinks it's a game. He skips after her and grabs her, grinning at her, twisting her arm a little so he can take a peek at her wrist. But he's not prepared for the ferocity of her resistance.

"Get off me, you ape!" she yells. Her face is red with exertion and anger.

Shocked, Mark releases her arm and stares after her as she hurries towards her house. She leaves him standing in the street and muttering words she can't quite hear.

"You're back, then," Helen calls as soon as Caz has slammed the door on Mark and the street outside. "I was wondering where you'd got to!"

There's something wrong with her mother's tone of voice. It's too singsong. Like someone pretending to be jolly. The kind of voice her mother reserves for when they have visitors.

Or a particular visitor.

A particular Maths-teacher visitor.

Helen has been out with Corky almost every night since she revealed him to Caz. It's as though that now the secret is out, they think they can relax around her.

"Hello, Caroline!" says Mr Corkhill. He's slightly red in the face. Caz dreads to think what they've been doing. The grin on his face is so wide it looks like a split in an overripe tomato.

It's unbelievable. He's on the sofa in his polyester shirt. There are small sweat-stains under his armpits. He has his shoes kicked off and his be-socked feet are on the sofa, near a cushion. Caz can't put aside the revolting thought that Corky might have spent the evening trying to get a feel of her mum's tits. She wants to go and rescue the cushion from Corky's socks. She wants to rescue it and stroke it and put it somewhere safe. *Isn't this all happening a bit fast*? she wants to say. *Shouldn't you be going out for at least six months before you get your feet up on our sofa?* Instead she says, "Hi," in a voice so tiny it barely comes out at all. Then she starts up the stairs.

Helen rushes out of the kitchen. She's wearing an

apron—an item she rarely ever puts on. "Where are you going, Caroline? We've been waiting for you so that we can all eat together." There is a note of accusation in Helen's voice.

"No one told me," Caz says, bristling.

"I thought it would be a surprise," her mother says.

A few minutes later, Helen serves up a dish of cauliflower cheese topped with strips of bacon. This, she declares, is Neville's favourite dish.

"Smells terrific!" he adds. "Yes, my favourite dish!"

It's not Caz's favourite dish. In fact it tastes like buttered cinders. Her jaw goes to work on the food, moving to and fro, but she can't make anything happen in her mouth: she's too busy staring at Neville Corkhill next to her, who seems so passionately involved with what is on his plate that he doesn't even notice.

The thing that bothers Caz most is how easily he has slotted in: almost with a little click of satisfaction as he lay on the sofa advertising his socks, or as he took his seat at the table. Like there were butt-shaped holes waiting for him on the sofa and the dining chair to slot his horrible large bottom into.

Click! Why all it would take would be for him to—

"Neville fixed that broken lamp in your room," Helen says, with a note of triumph in her voice. "And the dripping tap."

Caz's fork falls from her hand. The news is worse than she thought. He's doing the DIY. No doubt he's got a toolbox and an extension cable to go with his sweaty socks: the whole male catastrophe. *Neville* has already taken up position in the house. It's like suddenly, after everything was fine with just the two of them, now they have a ready-to-run plug-and-play *dad* in the house.

"Dripping tap?" Caz says, recovering her fork.

"And your broken lamp," Helen says, for extra emphasis.

Caz looks at her mother: there is an awful, tired grin on her face that seems to say, *Yes, Neville may have sweaty feet, a large, spreading butt, and a lousy taste in shirts, but isn't it great that he's got a screwdriver!*

Maybe Caz's low opinion on dads has something to do with the one who left her and her mum high and dry a few years back. Mostly what she remembers is tiptoeing around a big, moody presence, like having a bear in the house. Then seeing her mum so crushed when he left that she couldn't see why you would want to let anyone have the chance to do that to you again.

He wasn't exactly the kind of man who showed any affection, so there was little missed in the way of hugs and smiles and kisses. When her dad left there was a drop in income, and for a while the lack of money blew round the house like a cold wind. But they got used to it and they changed their spending patterns and it wasn't a hardship. And when he left, it was true there was no one to fix the things he'd always taken care of, like a blown fuse, but Caz had soon found out that there was no mystery about using a screwdriver, and she became the fix-up kid around the house. The truth was, at least for Caz if not for her mum, the old bear wasn't missed and she wouldn't want him back.

No sir, Caz just isn't ready for anyone to fill the Dad-shaped hole. She turns her gaze on her mother. She makes her eyes flash.

Helen doesn't give a damn about that. She just flashes her eyes right back at her. It's almost a conversation, but with bulging eyes and boiling irises instead of words.

Fortunately Neville, being of the male species, misses all of this eye-flashing. He does sense something, however. "So what did you get up to after school then, Caroline?"

"Cinema. I went to the cinema with a friend."

"More cauliflower cheese?" asks Helen.

"Lovely," says Neville, handing over his plate. "See anything interesting?"

"Pardon?"

"At the cinema. You said you went to the cinema."

Caz bristles. "I'm not lying, you know. When I say I went to the cinema, I mean I went to the cinema."

"Neville is only asking you what you saw, that's all," says her mother.

"I saw a film called *Red Juice*."

"Was it good?" Helen wants to know. She's raised her eyebrows almost to her hairline, trying to look the interested parent, though Caz knows it's just to impress Neville.

Neville has stopped munching his cauliflower cheese and is waiting for Caz to answer. He's pretending to look relaxed, but there's a red gleam behind his eyes that makes him look like a fox hiding in a hedge in order to pounce on a chicken.

"It was all right."

"I've heard about that film. I don't think it's suitable for a fourteen-year-old. Very violent." His head is still turned towards Caz, but he's looking sideways at her mum. "I'm surprised you let her go to see such things, Helen."

"Was nothing. A silly film," Caz says.

Neville ignores her. "Not exactly wholesome entertainment. Sex and gore. Not exactly suitable viewing for a teenage girl, I would have thought."

Helen's smile locks. Her lips are drawn back too far. It's not a Mum smile at all, in fact it's all wrong: it's more like the open zipper on a tart's jeans. "She is quite mature. . . ." she tries weakly.

"I think we can do better than that," Neville says. "What about the youth club I mentioned, Helen?"

"Youth club?" says Caz.

"Neville knows some people who run a youth club three nights a week."

"Through the church," Neville says brightly. "Of course it's really for the youth who do actually attend the church. But I could take you along to church with me on Sundays and that would make you eligible. The kids who go say it's really cool."

Something about that *really cool* makes Caz wants to guffaw. But she doesn't. She's too busy thinking about table tennis and Bible classes at this church youth club. What she wants to say is: *I'd rather have my toenails pulled out by an Iraqi terrorist; I'd rather have my teeth drilled and filled with nuclear waste; I'd rather have my leg hairs removed one by one with a pair of steel pliers. . . .*

That's what she wants to say. But what comes out is, "Nah."

Helen's zipper smile falls from her face and lands in her unfinished cauliflower cheese. "No need to be so rude, Caroline!"

"I'm not being rude. I'm not available on Sundays, as it happens."

"What do you mean by 'not available'?"

"I've got a job."

"Job? I don't know anything about a job! What job?"

"Collecting glasses."

"Glasses? Where?"

"Hell, where do you usually collect glasses, Mum?"

"You mean in a pub?"

"Well, I don't mean at the newsagents."

Helen is openmouthed. Neville looks at her and shakes his head, as if to say: *I don't know, this family is going to be a really big job for me.*

Helen decides to put her foot down, something she's not accustomed to doing, and when she does, it lands heavily. "No way. I'm not having you working in a pub, young lady."

"Since when did you show a scrap of interest in what I do? You spend all your life sleeping." Even before it's out Caz knows this is unfair. It's a catty remark designed to inflict the most damage on Neville's view of Helen. But there, it's said.

"Take that back," Helen says. "You just take that back, my girl!"

But Caz is already up from the table. "Got to go," she says. "I've got some *maths homework* to do."

She's halfway up the stairs when she hears Neville. "Leave her."

Caz isn't stupid. She knew all along she would have trouble explaining the idea of the glass-collecting job to her mother. In a way it's just as well that it came out when it did. If it hadn't, Helen would have tried to persuade her into a dozen less well-paid jobs. Babysitting. A paper round. Washing people's cars. Now it's out, she can maybe use it as a negotiating point.

Caz also realises she's going to have to give something big in return. Something very big. Something that might even turn her stomach, but which she can endure if she has to. She's already got her deal worked out before the soft knock on her bedroom door comes.

"It's Neville. Can I come in and talk to you?"

The door opens a little. Neville steps inside. He's careful to leave the door wide open, though it looks as though Helen has been instructed to stay downstairs.

"Look, I'm sorry," Neville says. "I never intended to cause an argument. I don't want you to think I'm coming here throwing my weight about. I think it must be difficult enough, having a new guy in your mum's life. Even worse if he happens to be one of your teachers."

Caz doesn't look up. "How did you meet?"

"Salsa dancing."

The thought of Corky doing the mambo with her mum makes her want to vomit. She says nothing.

"I just thought you'd like to give our youth club a try," he says.

"I'll come," Caz says. Just like that.

"What?"

At last she looks up at him. "I'll come to church with you on Sunday."

"Really? That's fantastic, Caroline. You've made me really happy!"

He has no idea how desperate she is. She has to get some money and find a way of getting rid of this curse, and if this is one of the things she has to do, then she's prepared to do it. "But in return, I want you to help me. I'm not irresponsible, and I want a job to earn myself some pocket money. Hard work never hurt anyone, did it? I'll need you to persuade Mum that it's okay for me to work in a pub."

His face falls. "I don't drink and I don't much care for people who do—"

"I won't be drinking! I'll be collecting empties!"

"It's not a good environment for a young girl."

"It doesn't seem fair!" Caz moans. "I've come halfway, but you won't!"

He looks out of the window, and she knows she's won.

"I'll see what I can do. I'm not promising anything."

"You'll talk to her?"

"I'll talk to her."

"Thanks, Neville," says Caroline.

CHAPTER ELEVEN
What's That Smell?

HOLY MOSES! What a church it turns out to be!

Hallelujah!

Caz walks in behind Neville and Helen, and the service is in full cry. Neville has already told them that they can arrive or leave whenever they like. Unlike a lot of churches, the service at the Free Movement Ecstatic Church doesn't have a specific start and finish time. It begins as soon as the first person arrives and ends when the last person leaves.

There is also a rule about women wearing a hat or a scarf to cover up their hair, which for some reason in this church is offensive to God. Helen has opted for a simple headscarf. Caz, who said she'd die rather than wear a headscarf, has gone for a beret belonging to her mother. Weird, yes, but at least, she thinks, it looks a bit arty. Though it doesn't seem fair to her that men can show off their dodgy haircuts or their shiny bald heads. As she looks around, there are some pretty bad male haircuts on offer. If women's hair is offensive, why not men's?

Not that Caz knows a lot about churches or has been inside churches much. She's attended a christening service, two weddings, and one funeral. At school, she's been inside large cathedrals for special services or remembrance days.

Church: she's just not big on it. She has to remind herself exactly why she's there. Every time she thinks about her curse, she unconsciously covers her wrist with her hand.

Though this church is nothing like anything she's seen before. To begin with, there is no big altar at the front, only a plain table with a simple wooden cross. No stained-glass windows. No candles. No bells and smells. Bare walls. No vicars in robes of any kind. In fact, there appear to be no less than three people conducting this service. Two men and a woman are standing up at the front and they are whipping up a storm, shouting things she can barely hear because the congregation keep shouting back at them.

"Don't worry," Neville says, "come on in."

"What are they doing?" Caz whispers.

Neville smiles. "Why, they're praising the Lord!"

Even Helen makes a face at Caz, but Neville, smiling and waving and shaking hands with various people in the congregation, leads them to some empty seats. Not that anyone is sitting, for the entire congregation is on its feet, shouting and clapping their hands and whooping and shouting "Hallelujah!" And "Praise!" And even whistling—wolf-whistling!—and singing, yes, a lot of them are singing.

It's just they are all singing a different song.

When Caz went to the cathedral for a school service, the vicar said "Hymn Number 365," and they all turned to the appropriate page and sang that hymn, or at least pretended to. Not here. Caz looks around at the faces of the people. There is a pleasing mixture of white and black people, but they all seem to have one particular thing in common: they all look like they get their clothes at the same charity shop.

A young white man standing next to her claps his hands and dances to a rhythm only he can hear. A large black woman rolls her eyes and flutters her fingers in the air, speaking gobbledy-gook. The noise is incredible. There are about sixty people chanting and whistling and "praising the Lord."

Caz has one thought: *I want to get out.*

"What are they doing?" she asks Neville.

"They're talking in tongues," Neville says. "I'll explain later."

Caz's sleeve has ridden up her arm, and in a moment of horror she realises that her tattoo is glowing again with a faint, silver light. She quickly pushes her sleeve back down.

She looks round at the people to see if anyone has noticed; they are focused on what is going on around them. But there, in the far corner, not joining in with the religious frenzy of the room, is a familiar figure wearing sunglasses. Caz feels a horrible scraping sensation deep in her belly. It's the woman who was also in the cinema. Fizz, from the tattoo parlour. Suddenly she seems to be everywhere that Caz happens to be, almost as if she's following Caz around. Fizz lifts her hand and waves lightly, as if with difficulty. Then she looks to the front of the room where the three church leaders—the perspiring men in polyester shirts and the woman in a huge floppy hat—are orchestrating this "talking in tongues."

"Don't look so nervous," Neville says to her, "it will pipe down in a minute."

In fact the noise is already beginning to subdue. Caz can actually feel the energy of the congregation dropping, like a sudden fall on a barometer, as people start to sit down. The three leaders at the front also collapse into chairs, looking pretty exhausted. Caz thinks maybe the reason they all wear polyester shirts is because they sweat so much, and polyester is easier to wash. She considers asking Neville about that later, along with her question about hair. Then she thinks maybe she should just keep them to herself.

She can't help stealing another glance at Fizz, whose sunglasses are trained on the front of the room, and as Caz looks back, something new is happening there. A tall man with a large friendly face and silver-grey hair, a man well into his sixties, has commanded the space at the front. He spreads his arms wide.

"Hallelujah, brothers and sisters!"

The congregation responds with a resounding "Hallelujah!" Some whistle. Some cheer.

"Elder Collins," Neville said. "He's really good."

"There is great and abiding love here today, brothers and sisters!" declared Elder Collins.

"Love!" "Praise the Lord!" "Great and abiding!" "It's the truth!"

"In the Lord we are strong, brothers and sisters. Strong!"

Several people bellow out the word *strong*. Caz begins to understand that this man is some kind of vicar, because he begins to preach. He doesn't seem to mind when members of the congregation echo his words or shriek or roar out phrases of their own. He continues to speak in beautiful but antiquated words.

"For are we not told that those who have hope in the Lord will renew their strength? They will soar on wings like eagles; they will run and not grow weary; they will walk and not be faint."

Someone shouts out, "Isaiah!" Another yells, "They will walk!"

But Caz temporarily loses interest in the preacher. She is far more curious about the presence of Fizz. Something about the woman scares her. It makes her mouth run dry. She can feel herself sweating.

Of course, it could be pure coincidence that Fizz had been in the cinema, but this hardly seems to be the kind of place where she would expect to find a lady tattooist. Meanwhile Fizz has settled into a seat, and with her being so small Caz can barely see her. All she can make out are her sunglasses and the tip of her nose.

It is while trying to sneak glances at Fizz that Caz becomes aware of another change in the temperature of the room. The congregation has gone almost silent. The mood has altered. Now they are only murmuring in response to the preacher, and his voice, too, has sunk low.

"We have a presence," says Elder Collins. "I sense that presence."

"Surely," someone murmurs.

"For where there dwelleth the Lord, so do his enemies muster. The instruments of darkness do so hate the light, and yet they cannot tear themselves away."

"That's right." "Indeed it is."

Elder Collins begins to prowl between the chairs, trailing his fingers, touching his congregation lightly as he passes, rolling his feet, scanning all the upturned faces as he moves between them.

"This is creepy," Caz whispers to Helen.

"Shh!"

"And that they cannot tear themselves away is their desire for the light, for they in their misery and their wickedness are but evil souls crying out for redemption from the midst of their agony." Elder Collins begins to move even more slowly between the members of his congregation. He seems to be almost sniffing the air, searching something or someone out.

"For even today . . ." His nostrils twitch as he slowly scans the rows of faces. "Even in this house of the light . . ."

He rolls his feet forward, scanning, scanning, twitching his nostrils. It seems to Caz that the people are waiting in terror for him to pick one of them out. They wait, breath bated, eyes bulging as they follow the tall man's stalking progress around the room. "Even in this tabernacle of worship do I detect something, right here, today, amongst us all."

Elder Collins's gaze falls on Caz. He makes his way slowly towards her, gently touching other members on the head or the shoulder as he moves. "I sense something," he says, his voice a strong whisper now. "I smell something here today. What is it I sense?"

Oh no, thinks Caz, *he's heading towards me!*

He's actually going to single me out!

And it's true. Elder Collins is reaching, pointing at Caz. "What is it I smell?" he says.

Caz looks in desperation, first at Helen, then at Neville. But her mother's face is twisted in a kind of horror, and Neville's face is paralysed. The church Elder gently probes his finger in the direction of Caz's forehead, but just as he is about to touch her, there is a rustle and a disturbance across the room.

Caz looks up. It is Fizz. She is standing up. In doing so she distracts Elder Collins, who instantly changes direction and swings his pointing finger towards the woman. "What is it I smell?" Collins says again. He stalks slowly across the room towards Fizz, and as he does so, she slowly lifts her hand towards her face.

Elder Collins raises his voice. "I . . ." he shouts, taking a step closer to Fizz.

Fizz flicks back the ringlets of her curly black hair. Her hand reaches up towards her sunglasses.

"*. . . smell . . .*" roars Collins, pointing hard now at Fizz.

All the congregation nearby are stepping away.

Fizz's fingers close round the frames of her sunglasses. She begins to remove them, very slowly.

"*. . . demons!*"

And as Collins screams the word, leaning into Fizz with his pointing finger, Fizz reveals her eyes, which are not eyes at all. Instead, where her eyes should be, there are black storms streaked by lightning and in which planets and moons shriek by at terrifying speed. The stormy holes crackle with an energy that in turn becomes a brilliant and blinding white sodium light, pulsing out across the room like a shockwave. The flash of light leaves Caz blinded and in total darkness and silence, in which she faints clean away.

CHAPTER TWELVE
Discouraging the Punters

THE SIGN IN the tattooist's window reads: WE'RE CLOSED. TOO BAD. SOD OFF. Caz tries to find a chink of uncovered glass to look through. It's hopeless. She can't see anything. There's not even a sign to tell them when the place might be open again.

"We'll come back tomorrow," says Lucy.

"Are you sure you can't remember that woman?" Caz says, still trying to peer through the window.

"Sure."

"She wore black clothes and sunglasses."

"How many times, Caz? If there was a woman there, I didn't see her!"

Caz gives up at the window. Every time she thinks about this woman Fizz, she feels a little ill. No one saw her at the church the previous day before Caz fainted. Now they are on their way to The Black Dog for an interview. Both girls carry plastic shopping bags into which they have stuffed their school uniforms. They changed in public toilets, substituting jeans and crop-tops for their school clothes.

Caz has told Lucy everything that happened at the church. When she came to the bit about seeing Fizz in the congregation, Lucy said, "Who?"

"The weird woman in the tattooist's," Caz had said.

And that's when Caz's world started to crumble. Because neither her mother nor Neville were able to recall seeing a woman fitting that description before Caz had fainted. She was certain that Elder Collins had been pointing at Fizz while he was screaming something about demons, and that the woman had taken off her sunglasses to reveal a burning white light. But neither her mother nor Neville knew what she was talking about.

In fact when Caz had come round, Neville and her mum had her sitting on a bench outside the church. Neville was trying to reassure Helen, saying that it was the excitement that had been too much. He said he had seen it happen before. People weren't accustomed to letting their feelings go in what he called "ecstatic ceremonies." Caz, blinking her eyes and looking round her, had wanted to say she was neither excited nor ecstatic. Terrified, yes; ecstatic, no.

The solution seemed to be to check with Lucy, just to make sure that she hadn't completely imagined Fizz. But

Lucy swore she didn't remember anyone from the tattoo parlour other than the biker-tattooist. Caz thought about asking Mark if he'd spotted the woman at the cinema that evening. She hadn't drawn his attention to Fizz for the simple reason that she would have had to explain to him how she knew her.

If Fizz *was* an ordinary *her,* and not a . . . Caz had put that thought away.

It had been Lucy's idea to return to the tattoo parlour to quiz the man about his girlfriend. But now that the place was closed, that line of enquiry was blocked.

A thought suddenly occurs to Caz: her tattoo seems to glow whenever Fizz is nearby. She wonders if the two things are connected.

"Leave it," Lucy says, swinging her plastic bag with her school skirt and blazer. "We'll be late for our interview."

When Lucy and Caz arrive at The Black Dog, it's closed. Its wide doors, painted fire-engine red and daubed with graffiti tags so near the floor they must have been put there by a three-year-old, have two steel bars across the front. There is no letterbox or doorbell that they can see. Even though all the windows are closed, there is a sour tang of stale beer and ciggie-rot leaking through the thick walls. A swinging sign above the door has a painting of a black dog baying at the moon. The sign creaks on its hinges and a breeze blows a scrap of filthy newsprint down the street.

"There must be a door to take deliveries," Lucy says.

She's right. There is a side door. It's also locked. Lucy thumps on the door.

After a few minutes a man in dire need of a shave sticks his head out of a window above them. Even from this distance they can see that his eyes are bloodshot.

"What are you, carol singers? If I throw you a quid, will you bugger off?"

Lucy looks at Caz.

"Let's go," says Caz.

"You said come for an interview at five o'clock," Lucy shouts. "Anyway, you don't get carol singers in the middle of June!"

The man scratches his stubbly beard with clawlike fingers. "June, is it? All right, I'll be down."

The girls wait outside until they begin to think he's not coming. Finally they hear some bolts drawn on the other side of the door. The publican, a man in dirty jeans and a lumberjack shirt, could be aged anything between twenty-four and forty-two. He rubs his face and stares at them with eyes like poached eggs.

It seems like he's not going to speak, so Lucy says, "Glass collectors."

A small light goes on in the man's eyes. "How old are you?"

At the same moment Lucy blurts that she's sixteen, Caz says fifteen. They both turn and look at each other.

The man sways on the step. "Walk round the block and come back when you're sixteen." He shuts the door on them.

"Idiot!" growls Lucy.

"We can't lie about it," says Caz.

"Do you think he meant what he said? About walking round the block?"

"I think he meant we should come back next year."

"I don't. I think he meant we should walk round the block. Come on."

With Lucy dragging the protesting Caz along the way they make one circuit of the local streets. A few minutes later they are back at the door. When Lucy knocks, the man opens the door instantly. "We've come about the glass-collecting job," Lucy says, as if she's never seen the man before.

"How old are you?" he asks them.

"Sixteen," says Lucy.

"Sixteen," says Caz.

"That's all right then." He waves them inside, and they follow him along a dimly lit hall stacked high with bottle crates and crisp cartons, into a darkened pub. There is no natural light. The publican goes behind the bar and flicks on a small lamp. One of the things the light illuminates, next to the bar taps and beer towels, is a glossy porn magazine. He pours himself a small beer and the weak electric light is reflected in the amber liquid. He takes a drink, then sniffs at them. "Can you come on Wednesday night?"

"Have we got the job, then?" says Lucy, smiling.

"Can you come on Wednesday night?"

"Yes," Lucy says brightly.

"Yes," Caz says doubtfully.

"You two still at school?"

"Yes."

"Wear your school uniforms."

"You're joking!"

"No, I'm not. It'll discourage the punters from putting their hands on you. Some of them, anyway." He smirks, lifting his upper lip on one side of his mouth. "Mind you, some of them will like it." He smirks again. And winks.

"You said four pounds an hour," Lucy says.

"That's right. "

"And we keep any tips," she adds.

"Tips!" the landlord guffaws at this. "The only tip you'll get in this pub is to be told what horse to back."

"And you pay for a taxi home for each of us."

"Joking, aincha?"

"If you want us Wednesday, you have to pay for a cab."

He takes a sip of his beer and regards them steadily.

"Well?" Lucy says.

"See you Wednesday, at eight," he says.

"And do we get our cab home?"

"I said see you Wednesday, didn't I?"

That much, at least, is settled. On the way out, the landlord remembers to introduce himself. His name is Frank.

"I'm Lucy and this is Caz."

"Eh? I thought you said your name was June."

"Forget it," Lucy says. "See you Wednesday."

Caz, of course, has to negotiate Wednesday with her mum. Obviously she's not about to mention that her potential employer Frank, the half-awake porn-reading landlord, is a sleaze. Helen only has to drive up to take a look at the joint herself. Caz is going to have to fudge where exactly she's going to be working. The thing is, there is this weird trade-off.

After the dramatic events of Caz's first visit to church, Neville has been talking to people. "Elder Collins was very sorry about what happened. About you fainting. He's very interested in meeting you."

"Meeting me?" Caz smells a rat. "Why would he want to meet me?"

"To reassure you. To let you know that you would normally be all right."

There is an increased pulse in Caz's wrist, inside the tattoo. She knows that Neville is lying. It's creepy, but it's that intuition again, that way of knowing, that ability to see through people that started as soon as the tattoo appeared.

"It's okay. I'm happy to be reassured by you."

"He's a great man," Neville says. "It really would be very good for you to meet him."

Caz looks at Neville. He's pretending to be casual about this request, but for some reason he really wants this meeting to happen.

"Why does Mr Collins want to meet Caz?" Helen asks.

Neville pretends to stifle a yawn. "No reason. He's interested in all young people. After all, young people are the future."

Lying again. Not about young people being the future. But hiding something.

"Okay," Caz says suddenly, "I'll see him." And while Neville is still looking surprised she adds, "But it can't be Wednesday because I start that job I told you about."

"Job?" says Helen.

"Glass collecting."

"I thought that was going to be weekend work."

"Yes. Wednesdays and weekends."

"Where is it again?"

Caz coughs slightly. She's glad for once that she's paid attention in her French lessons. *"Le Chien Noir,"* she says. "It's one of those trendy bars. You know." She waves a hand through the air.

It's a small lie. A half lie. Or at the very least, a deception. And just as she can tell when other people are lying, her own lies have become painful to her. Her tattoo actually begins to smart.

"Caroline, I'm really not sure about this."

"Well, if you're going back on your word about this, I'm going back on my word about meeting Elder Collins and going to church. That's all I can say."

And Helen and Neville look at each other. Caz hauls herself off her chair and goes out of the room. She doesn't want them to see the smug expression on her face, because she knows she's *got them*.

CHAPTER THIRTEEN
Rougher Than Dog-Rough

CAZ'S DIARY IS starting to get filled up, and not always in ways she would have liked. On Tuesday evening she has another date with Mark; on Wednesday she is collecting glasses at The Black Dog; on Thursday Elder Collins is visiting the house with his black Bible; and she is determined at some point to revisit the tattooist to sort out the mystery of Fizz.

One thing she won't be doing is the Creepy. In fact for her and Lucy both, it looks like their Creepy days are well and truly over.

But no matter how busy she is, there is another person she knows she has to see before glass collecting again at the pub. It's the one she can't bear thinking about. In fact the very thought of seeing this person makes her gag. But she can't see any way around it.

Her date with Mark turns out to be a double-date when Lucy shows up at the bandstand with Conrad. Everyone behaves as if this was agreed earlier, which it certainly wasn't. Caz shrugs. It's convenient, because it will stop Mark from getting too hot for her. He won't be so bold with the other two there.

The disadvantage is exactly the same: Caz won't get so hot for Mark, and *she* won't be so bold with the other two around. This is disappointing. Maybe she would like to get a little bold with Mark. Maybe.

Caz wants Mark, and yet she doesn't. Wants him to put his tongue in her mouth and she doesn't. Wants him to put his hand under her clothes and she doesn't. That's it. It's like living in a *can't-make-up-my-mind* pop song. Yeah yeah yeah.

She doesn't really know how it happened, but Lucy and Conrad are "going out," too. So that's it then: they're a foursome. Caz looks at Conrad, and she thinks he's trying too hard. His face is scrubbed to a shine and he's wearing stinky. It must be his dad's aftershave, because he hasn't started shaving yet. And *whoa*! It's so strong he must have put it on with a hose-pipe. Mark doesn't wear aftershave because Caz has already told him she doesn't like it.

Lucy has two new things: a bruise near her eye and a brand-new, expensive pair of trainers. Once more Caz doesn't ask. She doesn't have to: she knows that Lucy's dad gave her both. It's an old pattern. Lucy's dad drinks, belts her, buys her something flash. Lucy is always careful to make sure the teachers never notice, and most things can be concealed with a bit of makeup. They never talk about what a shit her dad is. Ever. Caz wishes they could.

The evening is not a great success. Mostly the couples stand diametrically opposite each other, the girls with their backs to the bandstand walls, deep kissing for vast stretches of time without coming up for air. An hour goes by without one couple acknowledging the presence of the other.

Things would be okay if Mark didn't have this habit of breaking off the snogging occasionally to kiss, instead, the back of Caz's arm. Normally this wouldn't be a problem, but Caz can't afford to let him see her wrist. She gets the idea he's deliberately trying to snuffle underneath the buttoned-up wristband of her blouse. It leads to a silly argument that brings the evening, for all of them, to an early close.

On Wednesday night, the girls ignore Frank's advice to go to The Black Dog in their school uniforms. Instead they show off their cropped tops and blue jeans. Caz hides her tattoo with a dozen thin bangles. Before they leave for the pub they apply eye shadow, eyeliner, and lippy.

When they arrive at eight the place is already full. There is a heavy-metal band playing, and Frank is behind the bar pulling pints and growling at his bar staff, who are all young women showing plenty of cleavage. Customers stand three deep at the bar waiting to be served. The decibel level of the band is enough to loosen the wax in the girls' ears. There's a swirling mist in the room from a dry-ice machine on the stage, but it's almost made unnecessary by the thick fog of tobacco smoke.

"Where the hell have you been?" Frank doesn't break his work, flicking taps and slamming full pints onto the bar. "I told you to get here for seven."

"Eight," Lucy roars. "You said eight!"

Frank doesn't even look at her. "Tables. Glasses. We need 'em. Go."

They look at each other, then go to work, squeezing between the drinkers to collect empties from the tables. Lucy shows Caz how the beer glasses will fit inside each other. They find trays for the rest.

It's hot, sticky, sweaty, and farty. Most of the customers wear denim or leather. Plenty of the men wear their hair in an outmoded style that Caz's mum calls a mullet. Some of the women, too. People are drinking like they've been told they've only got forty-eight hours to live. Half the people are watching the band and the other half, despite the wood-splitting volume, don't even seem to notice that a band is playing.

Caz thinks you'd have to be desperate to drink here. Then she reminds herself that you'd have to be even more desperate to work there. She thinks of the money and takes a deep breath.

Caz gets into trouble early when she reaches for an empty glass.

"Oi, jailbait!" roars a bald-headed monster with a goatee. "I hadn't finished that!"

Caz looks at the glass. It's got maybe a gnat's spit left in it. She hands it back to him and he makes a great show of draining the glass, even making his Adam's apple wobble.

"Now you can take it," he says, giving her an evil glare.

Someone puts their hand on Lucy's bum. She rounds on him. "Keep your dirty claws to yourself, mate!" she shrieks.

Cheers go up from nearby drinkers.

"Oh, I loike 'em feisty, I do," says the offender.

"Look at the state of you," Lucy says. "I've seen better hair on a toilet brush." This gets more cheers. She looks at Caz fiercely. "Don't take any shit."

They don't just have to collect the glasses, they have to wash them by hand, too, when the overloaded washing machine isn't fast enough. They get sent into the corridor to fetch crates of drinks, cartons of crisps, or buckets of ice from a grinding, rattling machine in the bottle room. The pub serves curry and chilli with rice, and they double as waitresses to carry orders to the customers. They don't stop working, and they don't get a break.

In her first three hours at The Black Dog, Caz gets propositioned three times, has five offers of dates by men who look like they've all just come ashore from an eighteenth-century prison ship, is pinched bruisingly hard on the bottom, has her hair tugged, is kissed by a woman, and is handed a folded five-pound note by a man so drunk he has lost the faculty of speech. At least Frank was wrong about tips.

The band stops just before eleven. Frank calls time

with an electrical bell so loud it reminds Caz of school. He drapes bar towels over his taps and pumps and refuses to negotiate with anyone about a late drink. It doesn't matter because some tables have lined three or four drinks on their table before time was called. They have twenty minutes to drink what they have, then it's up to the staff to take the drinks away.

Frank has most of his customers well trained. If anyone argues with him, he asks them if they want to see his baseball bat.

Miraculously, his customers sink the ocean of beer, wine, and spirits in the allotted twenty minutes, and the girls slip between the tables like ghosts, pulling in the empties almost unnoticed by the bleary-eyed, blinking, burping, booze-addled mob. There are just a couple of mean-looking stragglers who want to test the drinking-up laws. Lucy steps towards the table to ask for the glasses, but Frank intervenes. "I want your glasses, boys."

A youth with a shaved head and a forearm full of misspelled tattoos burps at him. His mate, dragging on a dead cigarette, twists his face into a smile. "Bollocks."

Frank leans in, resting a hand on each side of the small, round table. "See that girl?" He indicates Lucy. "She's my head girl. She's coming back here to get your glasses in exactly thirty seconds' time. If she gets any trouble, or any lip from you, you'll discover it's *showtime*." Frank leans back and looks at his watch. Then he walks away.

"Thanks for nothing!" Lucy says under her breath.

Frank pats her cheek playfully. "Don't worry. They're

already finishing their drinks." He has his back to the boys. He can't possibly know this. But as Lucy looks over his shoulder, she sees he's right. The boys are draining their glasses. They are on their feet, ready to leave the pub. "Go get 'em," he says.

When the last customers have been bundled outside and the doors bolted, Frank and his busty bar staff sit down to enjoy a drink themselves. The girls, however, are charged with feeding the used glasses through the washer before they can leave. It's midnight when they're done.

"We're finished," Lucy says. "We need our cab."

The staff all stop talking. "I didn't agree to a cab," says Frank.

"I'll spit in every one of those clean glasses," Lucy says. It's one of those remarks that comes out as a joke that might not be a joke.

"And me," says Caz.

Frank snorts and wipes his mouth with his sleeve. "Don't pee in your pants, girls," he says. "I'm joking. Your taxi is waiting right outside."

"When do we get paid?"

"Saturday. I'll pay you then. Come at eight."

"You mean seven or eight?"

"Hell, I said seven, didn't I?" Frank turns back to his staff, who all start chattering again.

Caz and Lucy leave by the side door. Out on the street, a cab is indeed waiting to take them home.

On Thursday Elder Collins has been invited to visit Helen and Caz at six thirty, after tea. He arrives on the button, driven by Neville. Caz looks out of the window to see them climbing out of Neville's car. Elder Collins, even though he must be in his late sixties, swings up the pathway full of energy and gusto, gripping his black Bible. Caz's heart sinks. The doorbell rings.

Caz has no idea why Collins has taken a special interest in her. She guesses that it's all part of Neville's plan to recruit her in the church. Maybe they want to get her down to the youth club. Whatever it is, it's just something she has to get through, like getting through an evening of collecting glasses inside that vinegar bottle called The Black Dog. Keep Neville sweet and he will support her: get the money, get rid of the tattoo, get rid of the curse.

Collins is welcomed in and offered tea by Helen, who has got the best cups and saucers out for him, not to mention ginger biscuits and a Bakewell tart. Caz waits on the sofa, knees drawn up under her legs. When Collins steps into the lounge, his sparkling eyes immediately fall upon her and his lips draw back in an approximate smile. "Ah, this is the young lady who is the talk of the town!"

Caz doesn't know anything about the talk of the town. Before she has a chance to say anything, Helen has invited him to sit in the armchair directly opposite and is plying him with questions about Bakewell tarts and how he takes his tea.

He sets down his Bible and pinches the creases at the knees of his trousers before settling back into the armchair. Collins answers all of the questions about tea and tart without taking his glittering eyes off Caz for a second. It's unnerving. Plus Caz understands that the smile is fraudulent. Like the lies and dishonesty she can detect in people these days, she can see that it's not a smile of warmth or humour or friendliness of any kind. It's a mask. The tingling of her tattoo is telling her this. She just doesn't know what it's masking.

While waiting for his tea, Collins once again straightens the presses on the trousers of his dark green suit and crosses his feet at the ankles. He wears highly polished plain black leather shoes. Caz doesn't know whether to stare back at him. What she really wants to do is stick out her tongue, but she manages to restrain herself. Instead she fiddles with the braid on a cushion and looks out of the window.

"Yes, talk of the tabernacle," he says jovially. "Excitement got a bit too much for you on Sunday, did it?"

She realises he's talking about her fainting. "I think it was a bit hot in the room," Caz says.

"A bit hot?" He leans back in his chair and folds his hands in his lap. "It does indeed get a bit hot."

The tea comes in. Caz knows her mum is nervous because the teapot is clinking on the wobbling tray. Collins accepts his tea and cake.

"Shall we stay or would you like to chat alone?" Neville asks.

"Whatever you're more comfortable with," Collins says generously.

Neville puts a finger on his lips as if to think deeply about the matter. "I think we'll leave you to it. Come on, Helen, we'll sit in the kitchen and give them some space."

"As you wish," Collins says as Neville pulls the door shut after him.

Caz plucks up courage to say, "What's this all about?"

"All about?" says Collins, faking surprise at the question. "Why, it's all about *you*!"

"So why are you especially interested in me?"

"Lovely girl! I'm not the one who is especially interested in you. It's God who is especially interested in you. God."

Caz is stumped to answer. She hadn't thought about God being especially interested in her. In fact she never really gives God a second thought. Her mother has never been much for religion, and neither has she. "Why?"

Collins picks up his Bible again and presses on its black cover with that enormous thumb of his. "Because He's chosen to come into your life, Caroline."

"But I mean, why the sudden interest. From God." Her own words seem ridiculous: talking about God as if God was a chap down the road who would pop his head round the door when he'd got a free moment.

"I can never explain to people how or why God chooses His moments. All I can tell you is that He has decided you need Him right now, and here He is knocking on your door. Will you answer the door, Caroline?"

Another ridiculous thing happens. Caroline can't help flicking a glance at the door to the room they sit in, even though she knows perfectly well that Collins isn't talking about *that* door. "I don't know," she answers.

"Well, I'm here to help you make up your mind, if you'll let me."

How can anyone keep their eyes on you for so long without looking away? is what Caz wants to know. It is creepy. She wants to tell him to stop. But Collins goes on to talk about the number of times that God came into people's lives just when they needed it. He also tells her a story about Jesus knocking on a door and being ignored. And after a while Collins's voice becomes a gentle hum, like a lazy buzzing of bees about the honeysuckle on a summer's afternoon, and although Caz only focusses on half of what he says, she finds herself unable to take her eyes off his eyes. In fact his eyes seem to grow rounder and larger as he talks.

It's a strange sensation. Caz tries to pay attention to what he is saying, but as his face grows larger and looms nearer, the farther and farther away his voice seems. And then he's looking at her oddly and she guesses that he's asked her a question of some kind. Caz shakes her head, as if thinking about whatever question he has put to her.

Collins frowns, and in the next moment he's on his feet and coming across the room towards her, reaching out with his hand, directing his fingertips gently towards her forehead.

She's not sure what happens next, but the instant Collins's finger comes into contact with her brow there is a sudden hiss, like water falling on a hot griddle. Or is it Collins himself hissing? Then he cries out and leaps back like he's just received an electric shock, examining his fingertips as if they've just been burned.

Caz looks at Collins, and he looks right back at her.

Then he nods slowly. "So that's it," he says. "Just as I suspected."

"Suspected what?" says Caz.

The door opens and Neville and Helen rush into the room. "What happened?" Helen wants to know.

"It's all under control," says Collins, holding his Bible aloft. "But I'm afraid to tell you that Caroline is possessed by evil spirits."

CHAPTER FOURTEEN
Don't Dance on My Shoes

IT'S BREAK TIME at school. Lucy, Mark, and Conrad are all standing by the bike sheds, eating potato shavings dunked in fat and sold in bright coloured packets as food. Caz makes her way over to them.

"Why the long face?" says Lucy.

The events of the previous evening are like a bad dream for Caz. She isn't about to tell any of them what happened, though she desperately wants to talk about it to someone. If she tells them about Elder Collins, she will have to fill them in about the church. And if she tells them about the dancing-singing-swaying-happy-clappy church, she will have to spill the beans about Corky the maths teacher and her mother. She blames her mother. Why couldn't she pick a Catholic boyfriend, or a Muslim? Or why does he have to be religious at all? Why couldn't she pick some conventionally dull bloke, one who spends his Sunday mornings washing his car instead of rolling his eyes and shouting at demons?

Though it looks like Mr Corkhill might well get his marching orders after the way Caz's mum had reacted.

"Well?" Lucy says, waiting for an answer.

"Dunno. Feel sick."

"Have a crisp."

Caz shakes her head as if Lucy has just offered her a clove of garlic to suck. She leans her back against the bike shed and presses the sole of her shoe against its wall. Out of the corner of her eye she can see Mark looking at her, but she doesn't acknowledge him. She would tell him, but it's all too much.

When Elder Collins had told her mother that Caz was possessed, Helen had got very angry. In fact Caz hadn't seen her quite so cross before. She'd opened the door and invited Collins to leave immediately. When Neville Corkhill had tried to get involved, she told him to go with his Bible-bashing friend. Neville had tried to reason with her, but Collins had persuaded him that they should leave immediately. Helen had slammed the door after them.

Then she had burst into tears. When she had recovered she blew her nose and apologised for bringing "that lunatic" into her life. Caz hadn't known whether her mum meant Neville or Collins, but she had said it was really all right.

Now, as she stands with her back to the bike shed, trying to ignore Mark's gaze, trying to play it cool, there is only one thing on her mind: she thinks Elder Collins is right.

She may very well be possessed by an evil spirit.

The bell goes to signal the end of break. And her next lesson is Maths.

She manages to get through most of it without any eye contact with "our Neville." The lesson is the usual gripping stuff. They are doing "bearings," and the lesson has only a few minutes to run. Then, while she is writing in her exercise book, she sees a faint glimmering from her tattoo. It begins to glow with silver-grey light. She quickly tugs her sleeve over her wrist and hopes no one spotted it.

The Maths classroom has an old-fashioned blackboard as well as a marker board. Neville prefers the old-fashioned things in life, and he chalks away on the board, murmuring as he writes, almost to himself:

A, B, and C are three ships. The bearing of A from B is 45°. The bearing of C from A is 135°. If AB= 8km and AC= 6km, what is the bearing of B from C?

As Caz watches her teacher's hand move across the board, she notices how the chalk cracks and splits at its point of contact with the board, spitting tiny little clouds of chalk dust as it goes. Almost like leaving trails of smoke behind it.

$\tan C = 8/6$, so $C = 53.13^\circ$
$y = 180^\circ - 135^\circ = 45^\circ$ *(interior angles)*
$x = 360^\circ - 53.13^\circ - 45^\circ$ *(angles round a point)*
$= \underline{262^\circ}$ *(to the nearest whole number)*

As she looks at the letters and numbers in the top-left-hand corner of the board, she sees something wrong. Maybe she's imagining it, she thinks. But the letters are giving off a kind of smoke. Grey, twisting strands of smoke, like you might see from a lighted cigarette, drifting from the blackboard. She has to look round to see if anyone else in the class has noticed this, but they are all staring ahead blankly at the board (not that it means that they are actually paying any attention, but at least they're pretending to be awake, thinks Caz).

She looks back at the letters on the board. Now they are streaming thick white bands of smoke, as if they have been branded into the blackboard by a hot iron just two seconds ago. And just as she is about to raise the alarm the first of the smoking letters—those in the top-left-hand corner—burst into flame. The orange flame licks at the board, burning it back at the corner to reveal something, almost like another room hiding behind the blackboard, but one gleaming with an almost blinding white light like the one she saw in the church. The entire blackboard has burned back, and in the middle of the fearful light, removing her dark glasses, is the woman Fizz. The very woman who has been haunting her. Fizz is moving her mouth, but no words are coming out.

Caz feels the blood drain from her face. She feels an ice cold wave wash over her. Her mouth goes dry and she senses an uncomfortable itching in her head, and words form in her mind, unheard but clear:

Accept it.

The shock of what Caz is seeing has left her paralysed. The woman's mouth stops moving and her hand is raised to remove her sunglasses, but in the exact moment that the sunglasses are removed, the bell for the next class rings loudly in her ear, and the image of Fizz with her sunglasses is gone. The words in her mind have flown. The flames licking at the board have vanished and the smoke has disappeared. All that remains is the blackboard and the formula for bearings that Mr Corkhill has scribbled there.

The other pupils, having gathered up their books, are already halfway out of the door. Caz is left behind, still gazing at the blackboard.

Mr Corkhill sees her sitting alone. He smiles. "Was there something you wanted to ask me, Caroline?"

Caz fumbles with her books. She races from the room without giving him an answer.

Is Elder Collins correct? Is Caz possessed?

Caz thinks she must be.

After Corky's maths lesson she locks herself in a toilet stall, leaning her face against the door, trying to fight off her panic. Whenever she thinks of the woman's face she feels real terror. It's like she's walking across a flimsy rope bridge suspended across a lake of fire, and any moment it could go. She wonders if maybe the church *can* help her after all.

Her mother had been outraged. Helen had regarded the idea as so ridiculous she'd even been prepared to give Neville his marching orders. Caz had never seen her mum be so strong. If it hadn't all been so upsetting it might have seemed comical to see the two men bundled out of the house like that.

But she knows that her mother was just protecting her. It seems to Caz that it would be too much of a coincidence that this business has happened at the same time as the arrival of the bracelet. Still shivering, she wonders if some spirit, some demon has wormed its way into her, maybe tapping into the vein that stands strong and blue in the pale skin of her wrist. Maybe that's where it went in: through the bloodstream. How big is a demon? Maybe it's microscopically small. Maybe one could go in your ear. She doesn't even want to think about it. Anyway, none of it makes sense, because she knows it all has something to do with the bracelet.

And the demon is appearing to her, more and more.

Caz knows that the only way to find out what it means is to go back to the place where she first encountered the bracelet.

She's got to go back to that house. She's got to go back to talk to Mrs Tranter.

Caz resolves to pay a visit to the old woman over the coming weekend. But she's scared. Actually, she's not scared: she's terrified. She's come to think of Mrs Tranter as some kind of a witch or a sorceress. The idea of going to see the old woman makes her tremble.

She thinks about taking someone with her. She would ask Lucy, but she thinks that might make the whole thing worse, especially if Lucy decides to be aggressive on her behalf. She's got to somehow talk the old woman round and persuade her to lift this curse. She would like to ask Mark, but that would mean explaining the whole thing for him.

There's no one. It's something she will have to face alone.

Before that happens she has other things to worry about. Like glass collecting at The Black Dog this evening. She even has to turn down the offer of a date with Mark because she's working. Sarah Cannon, who is in the same Maths group as Caz, is having a party and Mark wants to take Caz along. Sarah's parents are going out for the evening. It will be a giant snog festival. What's more, Sarah fancies Mark, big-time. She'll be all over him like a rash.

But she has to go to The Black Dog. She has to go to The Black Dog to earn the money. She has to earn the money to get the laser treatment. She has to get the laser treatment to remove the tattoo.

This time Caz and Lucy turn up at seven instead of eight. The pub is not quite as full as it was on Wednesday, but more customers arrive at the same time they do. A band is setting up equipment on the stage. A big fat man with hair dangling halfway down his back is bending over an amplifier, showing the crack of his bum.

"You're an hour early," Frank says. He looks like he's just woken up again. "I told you to come at eight."

"Seven," yells Lucy. "You said seven."

"I'm not paying you the extra hour."

"Right," says Lucy. "Pay us for Wednesday, 'cos we're leaving."

Frank flicks a beer tap and pours a pint of beer in a glass. He holds the glass up to the light, squinting at it doubtfully. "Does that look cloudy?" he says to Caz. "What the hell. Your mate doesn't know when I'm pulling her leg, does she?"

"Neither do I," says Caz.

"You can start by getting some of these glasses washed," says Frank.

After half an hour, Frank comes into the bottle room with a blackboard that stands on the pavement outside the pub. "Go and put this outside, near the door," he says to Caz. "You carry on washing."

It's heavy. She drags it through the pub and out of the front door. A customer holds the door for her as she drags it outside. She opens the legs of the board and stands it out on the street. The pavement is a little uneven and the board wobbles. Caz finds a piece of broken brick and shoves it under one of the legs to make it stable. Satisfied, she turns to go back in. Then she does a double-take on what is written on the board in coloured chalk:

TONIGHT'S SPECIAL ATTRACTION:
TOPLESS GLASS COLLECTORS

After a moment's thought, Caz goes back inside. Frank looks up but keeps a straight face. One of his barmaids grins and turns away. They obviously think Caz hasn't noticed.

"All right?" says Frank.

"Fine," says Caz.

She returns to the bottle room and says to Lucy, "See if you can find where Frank keeps his coloured chalk, will you?"

"Why?"

"Tell you later."

After a few moments Lucy returns from the bar with the chalk. Caz uses the side door to steal out onto the street. Within a couple of minutes she's back.

"What are you up to?"

But Caz doesn't get a chance to tell Lucy. Frank appears with instructions for the evening. Friday, he tells them, is always a big night.

And so it is. By eight the place is heaving like a rugby scrum. The bar is three-deep again, and foaming pints and cocktails fizzing like bombs are passed overhead and deep into the pub crowd. It's hot, sweaty, and smoky. Tonight's band are called Dirty Noyze, and they burst into their first number with no introduction. It's so loud Caz thinks it might loosen the filling she has in one of her back teeth. She certainly can't hear the glasses clink as she collects them in interlocking towers resting across her shoulder.

The good thing about Dirty Noyze going off like a jumbo jet on the tarmac of a runway is that she doesn't have to listen to what the punters are saying to her. Some of them smile, some leer, one even waggles his tongue at her; some whistle, some coo, and one blows kisses. Some speak to her, some shout, and one sings in her ear. She floats above it all. It's a wall of sound, and she's put herself on the other side.

It's another hour before Frank appears in the bottle room while both girls are putting glasses through the machine and cleaning ashtrays.

He tugs Caz by the hair, but gently, playfully. "Very good," he says. "I'll have to watch you."

He goes out again. "Huh?" says Lucy.

Caz explains that she changed the sign board on the street to:

TONIGHT'S SPECIAL ATTRACTION:
Frank gives blow jobs with every order over £10

Lucy returns. "You didn't!"

"I did."

"What do you think of him? I can't work him out."

"Me neither."

Then Frank returns to yell, "Are we getting any work out of you two silly bitches? Get a bleedin' move on!"

It's about fifteen minutes before time when Caz runs into some serious trouble. There's an alcove at the back corner of the pub. It leads to a cupboard door where mops, buckets, and disinfectant are kept. One of the girls' less fun jobs is to mop up serious spillage, vomit, or both, a task they've already been called on to perform. The alcove is partially shielded by a cigarette dispenser and a gambling machine.

The way through to the door is always a squeeze, more so when anyone is using one of the machines. When a customer throws up near the stage it falls to Caz to get the mop and bucket. But there's this guy in the way.

He's a tall bloke with dirty, curly, mouse-brown hair and a goatee. Caz noticed him looking at her when she was working her first night. Her first thought about him was that he could do with a good scrub. He looks like he went to a Glastonbury festival on a very muddy year and never managed to get changed.

He takes a sip from his beer bottle as Caz squeezes through. He puts his mouth close enough to her ear for her to hear the words, "Where ya goin'?" Or something like that. Caz ignores him, but all he has to do is stick his knee out to stop her from passing.

"Let me through, please."

He ducks down to her level, offering her his ear, making out he can't hear her because of the music. So she repeats herself.

He beckons her nearer so that he can speak in her ear this time. She leans in, and well, it's an old trick, but he mashes his beery lips against her cheek. Caz smiles a hard, thin smile and forcefully pushes past him to get the equipment. On the way out she has the same struggle. This time he digs his hand inside the waistband of her jeans. She wriggles away from him, but his fingernails scratch her skin.

It only takes her a few minutes to clean up after the drunk, and when she goes back with her bucket of slops and vomit, he's still there.

"C'mere," he says. He's pissed and he's drooling beer. His eyes are half closed. He lunges for her but she dodges past him, even though she's tempted to throw the bucket of slops his way.

There's a sink and drain in the tiny closet. While rinsing out the bucket she hears the door slam behind her. When she turns she realises he's in the closet with her.

"Hey," he says, all big smiles.

There's barely room for one person to stand upright in the closet. He's practically standing on her shoes. "Get out of my way."

"Whoa! Slow down! Let's have a party!" He makes to dance to the beat of the loud music on the other side of the door.

Caz thinks about whether the mop would be a good weapon. But the closet is so narrow she wouldn't get a chance to wield it, and while she's still thinking about it, he's on her, trying to kiss her. Caz struggles, but he's strong as well as drunk. He grabs her breast and squeezes it hard. She tries to hit him, but with one hand he grabs both of her wrists and twists them over her head. With his free hand he pops open the button of her jeans.

The door opens and the wall of sound comes crashing in, along with someone else. It's Fizz, in her dark glasses. The man hasn't even noticed. Fizz grabs his wrist, twists his arm up behind his back and Caz hears a sickening crack of bone fracturing. The scream from the man is so loud that even the band onstage must hear it.

Whether or not they do, they carry on playing. Most people in the pub are utterly unaware of what is happening in the corner, but six or seven people have now gathered round the man writhing in agony on the floor.

Within seconds Frank is on the scene.

Caz is shocked. Her hands are still somewhere in the air. "He pushed me in the cupboard!"

"He did what!" Franks roars. He grabs the man on the floor by his hair and pulls him to his feet.

"My arm! My arm!" cries the man.

Frank is already dragging him though the crowd. "Nobody touches my girls, you shit! Hear that? Nobody touches my girls!"

Caz meanwhile looks round for Fizz. But she's gone. Caz sees Frank bump open the door and fling the groaning man out into the night. He doesn't seem to care where the guy lands. He just pulls the door shut, wipes a bead of sweat from his brow, and makes his way back over to Caz.

"Bottle room," he says.

Caz wipes her hands on a towel and follows Frank out to the bottle room, where they find Lucy loading the glass-washer.

"You all right?" Frank asks Caz.

"Yes."

"You decked him, didn't you?"

"No. It was . . . a woman. She grabbed his arm."

"What woman?"

Caz shakes her head.

"What you looking at?" Frank snarls at Lucy.

"Nothing!"

"Right, the pair of you. Let's have some fucking work done. We're trying to run a pub here."

Caz notices that the tattoo on her wrist is glimmering faintly.

At the end of the evening, when the punters have gone, the bar staff are enjoying their after-work drink. While Lucy and Caz are waiting for their cab, Frank asks one of the barmaids to say what she saw.

It's Liz, a bottle blonde with bad teeth and bad tattoos on her shoulders and arms. She's friendly, though, and is always kind to the girls. Liz stubs out a cigarette. "I just looked up and saw Caz pushing him to the floor. Well done, girl, I say."

"What about this woman Caz mentioned?"

"I didn't see no woman," Liz says. "Only Caz twisting his arm."

The taxi driver sounds his horn outside.

Before they leave Lucy plucks up the courage to ask Frank about their wages.

He looks up from his glass of beer. The bar staff all fall silent. "Next week. I'll pay you next week."

Caz and Lucy look at each other, before Caz speaks. "Is it going to be like this all the time? You string us along and never pay us?"

"Take it or leave it." He lights a cigarette with a Zippo lighter, and you can hear the tiny metal clink of the lighter cap as he closes it and turns back to his table.

"We'll leave it," says Caz.

Frank has his back to them now. "What's that on the bar?"

Lucy turns and sees two brown envelopes with their names on. She opens her envelope and finds the cash for Wednesday and tonight. The figure has even been rounded up, so there's a small bonus. Lucy passes Caz the other envelope.

"Taxi is waiting," Frank says. "Learn to take a joke."

Then as they leave Frank shouts, "Oi, you!"

They turn back and Frank is leaning across the table. His arm is fully outstretched and he's pointing his finger at Caz.

"What?" says Caz.

But Frank doesn't answer. He just points and stares at her. His bar staff start talking amongst themselves again, but Frank doesn't stop pointing and staring. He's still pointing when Caz and Lucy let the door close behind them.

On the journey home, Caz gazes out of the taxicab window. Something strange has happened. She's still terrified of this demon who is stalking her. But where she had started to think of it as something that might harm her, tonight it actually protected her. She's confused: confused and afraid.

"You're miles away," says Lucy.

"Huh?"

"Miles away."

CHAPTER FIFTEEN

When Soap and Water Is Not Enough

CLUTCHING HER MUM'S mobile phone for security, Caz stands at the hate-gate to number 13 Briar Street, trying to summon enough courage to knock on the door. She feels dreadful, sick to the stomach, exhausted. She's had a bad night, unable to sleep, tossing and turning just at the thought of coming face-to-face with the vile Mrs Tranter.

Can it really be possible that Mrs Tranter is some kind of a witch, an evil sorceress with dangerous powers? The hag knew what she was doing when she clamped the bracelet on Caz's wrist that night. Caz looks at the tattoo. It's dull. Standing outside the woman's house doesn't cause it to shine. If Fizz is Mrs Tranter's demon, she doesn't live at 13 Briar Street.

Caz has the money she made from working in the pub, plus her savings. She's ready to offer it to Mrs Tranter if it will do any good. She knows this is a desperate idea, but what else can she do? She bites hard on her thumb, turns, opens the gate, and makes her way up the narrow path.

Each step is heavy. It all looks a little different: the gate and the front door seem to have had a smart coat of paint since she last looked at the house. The front garden, too, has been tidied. The borders are well tended and the small front lawn has been trimmed. Where it had formerly been neglected and overgrown, someone has decided to take a new pride in its appearance.

Caz stands at the door trembling. She has a taste of metal in her mouth and she thinks she might be sick at any moment. She glances up and down the street. Thinking she might faint, she sways slightly. At last she summons the strength to reach out and press the bell.

It's an old-fashioned vibrating bell, and it reverberates in an angry buzz on the other side of the door. It makes the house sound empty. Caz feels a sigh of relief sweep through her at the thought that she can turn away, that the old woman is out and she doesn't have to look into her eyes.

But just as she's about to turn from the freshly painted door she sees a figure appear behind the frosted glass, and her stomach rolls. An arm, distorted by the glass, reaches to open the door. There's a fumbling with the catch and then the door is opened just a crack.

Mrs Tranter's stormy brown eyes peer through the crack at her. Caz wants to die. Her heart races. Her tongue sticks to the roof of her mouth. She can actually hear her own blood banging in her ears and she thinks she might pass out.

The old woman stares at her. She says nothing, and Caz seems to have lost the power of speech. "Oh," says Mrs Tranter after an age. "I wondered when you'd be round here. You'd better come in."

Caz takes a seat in the living room, perching on the edge of an old and faded leather chair, her eyes on the door waiting for Mrs Tranter to reappear, wondering if she shouldn't just make a break for it and escape. The old woman is making her a cup of tea. She asked, and Caz said no, but the old woman went ahead as if she'd said yes. Though Caz is certain she's not going to drink it. She's sure that the old woman will put something weird in the tea.

She checks out the room. While she's waiting for the old woman to return, she is sure that something has changed. Of course she only saw it in the dark that night, but the place feels different. That damp smell has gone. The place has a cleaner, fresher air to it. It seems to have been fixed up and decorated recently. Same with the hallway: the aspidistra plant is still there, but where Caz was expecting the smell of sweet decay that was so strong on the night of the Creepy, the house has had a spring clean.

Mrs Tranter returns with her tea tray. She's wearing a big fluffy pair of pink slippers that make her feet look huge. The china cups and saucers rattle in her shaky grip. Mrs Tranter sets the tray down on the table. "Yes, I wondered how long it would be before you'd have the gumption to come here. Milk and sugar?"

"No. I mean, just milk, please."

"It's all right. I know what you're thinking, and the answer is no. I'm not a witch. I haven't put anything nasty in your tea."

"I wasn't thinking that."

Mrs Tranter poured the tea and handed her the cup. "There's no point you telling me lies. Even though I haven't got it anymore, I can still see your lies. Yours and anybody else's. That ain't gone away at all."

Caz blinks at her.

"Yes," Mrs Tranter says. "That's one of the things as does come along with it." She sits down with her own cup of tea. She pours a little of it into the saucer and she laps at it, like a cat, and then sucks it up with a slurping sound.

Caz is speechless. All she can do is stare at the old woman. And it seems to her that something about the old woman has changed, too. She'd seen her more clearly around the neighbourhood before the night of the Creepy, at the supermarket, and in the street. But now she seems healthier. She's put on a little weight, and her face is not so drawn. Her hair is different. Where it was lank and straggly she's had it permed into a head of tight curls. Not what you'd call glamorous, but a marked improvement on what came before. She even looks ten years younger.

"What you staring at, girl? Is it my hairdo? I just had it done last week. Long time since I had a hairdo. Long time since I had enough money to have a hairdo. Or to buy myself some nice slippers. But then my luck seems to have changed lately, and why d'you think that is? Aren't you going to drink that tea I made you? There's nothing wrong with it, I tell you. And what's more you can tell if I'm lying about it."

It's true. Caz can tell. She sips her tea.

Mrs Tranter seems to relax a little. She nods with approval, tips a little more tea into her own saucer, and slurps at it noisily.

"Show me your wrist."

Caz puts down her tea, unbuttons the sleeve of her blouse, and holds up the tattoo for Mrs Tranter to inspect. Mrs Tranter squints at it, then quickly loses interest.

"Will it come off?" asks Caz.

Mrs Tranter shakes her head. "Not with soap and water it won't."

"How will it come off?"

"That would be telling, wouldn't it?"

"Will you tell me?"

"Might. Might not."

"Please take it back! Please!"

"Ha! You're a good 'un! Why would I take it back? Now my luck has changed. After I got rid of it to you, I got a visit from the Council, who came and inspected my house. Can you see how they've been fixing up for me? New heating system. Banister rails so's I can get up and down the stairs properly. Did my garden, too, and painted the front door. Then a relative of mine drops dead and leaves me a bit o' money. What a time I'm having after all these years of misery. Folk even look at me differently now. They speak, some of 'em. Speak! So why would I change all that? Why would I take it back from a girl who comes in the night to steal things from a defenceless old lady?"

Caz wants to protest that she wasn't out to steal that night, but she can't find any words. She can't speak because she's crying. Tears stream down her face. She wipes them away with the back of her hand.

"Yes, got more than you bargained for that night, didn't you? And those tears won't work on me, young lady. Not at all. And they won't wash it away, neither. You've got it now. You live with it."

Caz pulls it together. She stops crying. "Won't you at least tell me what's going on?"

"It's all there for you to see, isn't it? Have you still got the bracelet?"

"No! It disappeared. At first I couldn't get it off and then it just seemed to slip off my hand when I didn't notice. I've no idea where it is now."

"Oh, I daresay it will turn up when the time is right."

"Am I possessed?"

"What? What's that you say?"

"There was this man from the church. He put his hand on my head and said I'd been possessed. Is that what happened to me when you put the bracelet on?"

"I don't know what you're talking about. Neither do them churchy types know anything about it, either. Have you seen your other?"

Caz doesn't know what she means. She shakes her head.

"Well, it's different for different people. Whatever it is, you're stuck with it, and good luck to you, but it ain't my problem anymore, is it?" Mrs Tranter pours the last of her tea into her saucer and slurps it down.

Caz feels a sudden stab of anger. She gets out of her chair. "What have you done to me? Why won't you tell me anything? You're the only person who can help me!"

Mrs Tranter only seems amused—in a cruel way—by this outburst. She's enjoying seeing Caz's anguish. "Help you? Maybe I shall. But you've got to earn that help. And if you earn it, then maybe I will help you."

"What do you want me to do? I'll do anything!"

"Well, the kitchen floor needs a good scrub for starters."

"What?"

"And after that I've got some washing that needs taking to the laundrette. That'll keep you going for most of the afternoon, won't it?"

"Laundrette?"

Mrs Tranter gets to her feet. She puts both Caz's and her own cup and saucer on the tray and carries them to the kitchen. Over her shoulder she says, "Or you can go home, and then you shall know nothing, shall you?"

CHAPTER SIXTEEN

Only If You Show Me Your Thumb

LATER THAT AFTERNOON Caz calls Mark to explain that she's not going to be able to meet him. He's not a happy bunny. Because she's working at The Black Dog in the evening she can't see him that night, and they'd arranged to spend some time together in the afternoon. She finds it hard to explain to him what exactly it is that she's doing. How can she say she's scrubbing floors and toting the laundry without giving him the whole story?

So of course he gets the wrong idea. "Look," he says, "if you don't want to go out with me, just say so. Only don't mess me around."

"It's not that!" she almost shouts. "I'm just tied up with things."

"So when will I see you?"

"Tomorrow. In the afternoon. I promise."

"Have you finished that floor yet?" It's Mrs Tranter, yelling at her.

"Who's that?" says Mark.

"No one. I'll talk to you tomorrow."

She cuts Mark off. Mrs Tranter hands her a bag full of laundry. She makes a big fuss of counting out the exact coins that Caz will need to wash it and dry it at the laundrette.

It's almost two hours later when Caz returns with the washing. She dumps it on the table. "That's enough of that. You can't treat me like Cinderella. Now you'd better tell me something that I need to know."

"Calm your nerves, young lady. You're always for getting het up and angry and it shall do you no good. I'll tell you what I know, but there's something I want you to do while I'm telling you."

"I'm not doing any more of your slave work."

"It's not slave work." Mrs Tranter removes her slippers, and then slips off her ankle socks. "I want you to trim my toenails."

"*What?* You must be joking."

The old woman crosses the room and opens a drawer, returning with a pair of steel nail clippers. "You can do it while I'm talking."

Caz is left looking at Mrs Tranter's toenails. They are cracked and yellow. In all the jobs Caz has ever considered, this ranks as probably the most disgusting.

She snatches the clippers from the old woman's hands

and kneels down in front of her. "You'd better start talking or I'll take off more than just your toenails."

Mrs Tranter seems to enjoy the threat. She presents her toes for Caz, relaxing back into her chair and folding her hands. "I've never told this story to anyone. And I've long awaited the day when I could. It goes back a long time. Almost fifty years. I was only a little older than you are now. And I did something I shouldn't. I'm not telling you what it was, 'cos that's my business. All you need to know is that I got the bracelet clamped on my hand pretty much the same way you did.

"And would it come off? Just as you have found. And then all by itself, it goes, and it leaves a mark behind, a mark you can't let others see, as it makes no sense. And no amount of scrubbing with carbolic soap will take the mark off you. And no amount of praying, neither. That's it: you're marked. You're the one who has to carry the mark.

"You know, don't you, that this bracelet is very old. Older than I can say. Who can tell how many owners it has had. Twenty? A hundred? Two hundred?

"But then your luck begins to change, and for the worse. Because with it comes the sight. Yes, you can see straight into people's hearts. You've found that out, haven't you? You know when they're false, when they lie, when they cheat. You've just started. It gets stronger. And let me tell you this: you won't want to see it all. The more you find out about people, the more you wish you couldn't see them naked in this way.

"And because they can tell you can see through them—for you can't hide it forever, as I tried to—they begin to shun you. Because they see something in you. And they fear it, they do.

"I was never married, you know. I was a good-looking gal when I was young. Prettier than you, oh yes. I could make the men's heads turn. They were all after me, they were. I had a head of hair in those days. But I couldn't keep a boyfriend, far less a husband. Because I could see into their hearts, and when I saw what was there I didn't want them, and they didn't want me.

"And it's not just the men who shun you. It's the women, too. And what happens to people like me? They become a lonely old woman in the neighbourhood, laughed at, abused by everyone, teased and tormented. Preyed on by young girls who break into the house to steal what little you have."

Caz's clippers crack loudly through a horny old nail. The nail clipping goes shooting across the room. She looks into the woman's eyes. "We weren't stealing."

Mrs Tranter squints at her. "No, I see that. You were just causing mischief. Tormenting people weaker than you. You young people just think everything is a joke and a laugh. And now you're learning that it ain't. Well, that's what happened to me. No one would speak to me from one day to the next, unless to torment me. But then you came along, and you gave me my chance."

"Chance? What chance?"

"Finished? Pick that bit o' nail up off the carpet. We're done for today."

"But I've got lots more questions," Caz complains. "What's this about a chance?"

But Mrs Tranter is slipping her socks back on, and her vile pink fluffy slippers. "It's time for you to go. I'm tired. You shall come another day and help me out a bit. Here and there."

She gets up and walks to the front door, holding it open for Caz to leave.

And it seems only moments later when the door to The Black Dog opens and Caz has to face even more work. She's exhausted before she begins. Not just because of the floor scrubbing and the laundry for Mrs Tranter, but through thinking about all that was said. If Mrs Tranter is a witch she's not a very scary one. The more time that Caz spent there, the more she just seemed to be a lonely and eccentric old woman. And Caz doesn't feel she learned much, either.

The evening drags. Caz collects and washes glasses, but she's barely there.

"Are you okay?" Lucy asks.

"Crack us a smile, then," says Frank.

"Everything all right, Caz?" says Liz the bottle-blonde barmaid.

Yes, yes, yes. Everything's all right. Why wouldn't it be?

But every time a customer reaches out helpfully with an empty glass, she thinks: *Would that one work? If I had the bracelet, could I just clamp it on his hand?* Or on the occasion when some drunk guy "accidentally" brushes her butt as she squeezes by: *Would that be the time?*

But first she's going to have to find the bracelet.

She gets another offer of marriage. Seems like every night at The Black Dog someone wants to marry her. With each beery offer the joke becomes less funny. It occurs to Caz that working in The Black Dog is a great way to meet men if you're desperate to get married, and you don't mind if your future husband looks like the result of close inbreeding.

She starts to learn to dish it out a bit, like Lucy does. She's learned something in school about the importance of the opposable thumb in evolution.

"Hey, show us your tits!"

"You show me your opposable thumb first."

But that goes above most of their heads, so she changes it a bit.

"Oi, show us your tits!"

"I'd ask you to pass me that glass but you haven't got an opposable thumb."

Still some of them have to have it explained. So she tries new lines: "You wouldn't need contraception with your personality, would you?"

Frank hears her say this to one of his customers and he nods in approval. "You're catching on," he says.

She doesn't say anything to Lucy about what she learned at Mrs Tranter's that afternoon. She's not sure why.

On Sunday morning her mum has some news. It appears that Neville has been round, trying to put things right. He's back on the scene.

Caz tries to gently talk her round. She tells her mother that she could do better than Neville. Someone more fun. Someone less stuffy.

"Where am I going to meet someone?" Helen says, not for the first time.

The Black Dog, thinks Caz. Then she thinks: *Maybe not.*

"Anyway, Neville wants the three of us to spend today together."

Caz flips. "I'm not going back to that freak-show church of his!"

"Not the church. After he's been to church he wants to take us out in his car, on a picnic."

"I can't. I'm seeing Mark."

"But you saw Mark all day yesterday. Don't I get five minutes with you?"

Caz is about to protest that she never saw Mark at all yesterday. But she manages to stifle her own words because she realises she would have to explain how she came to be clipping a disgusting old lady's talons. Instead she marches out of the door and slams it behind her before storming upstairs.

Yet Caz is not a slam-and-storm type of girl. In fact, that sort of behaviour makes her feel stupid and childish. It's just that it's all becoming too much, and there seems to be no one with whom she can speak about all this. No one, that is, who would make any sense of it.

Just when she's about to burst into tears her mum knocks on the door and comes in. "It's okay, Caroline. I'll tell Neville you'd already made other arrangements. You go ahead and see Mark."

She meets Mark in the park, down by the river. It's a glorious afternoon. Swans glide by, rippling the water with their wake. Sunlight flakes through the trees. They sit on a bench near the water and after a while they kiss, ignoring passersby. Caz clings to him. She likes the way Mark kisses, the way he gently explores her mouth with his tongue. She likes the way he smells, too. They feel right together, and with everything else in her life falling apart, for Caz it's a moment of happiness in the sunlight.

But something's wrong. She feels it. She doesn't know how to ask him.

When they break from kissing, Caz mentions that she thought Lucy and Conrad might show up.

"No," Mark says. "I asked Conrad not to bring her here today."

"Oh?"

Mark looks away. A mallard with its glistening blue-and-green plumage comes flying in low, landing on the water in a great clattering. "I wanted to be able to talk to you."

"Oh? Sounds heavy."

It is heavy. She knows it is because he won't look at her.

"I really like you, Caz."

"I really like you, Mark."

Now he turns to look at her. His blue eyes are wide open. He's struggling with this.

She says the big word for him. "But."

He looks away again, and there, it's all out in the open. He's brought her here today to dump her. That's why he didn't want Lucy and Conrad around.

Then it comes out all at once. "You're just so distant! You run hot and cold on me. Sometimes when I'm with you it's like you're in a world of your own. Then I don't know what you're doing half the time. Like yesterday: you wouldn't tell me where you were or who you were with, so it was obvious you're keeping some big secret from me."

"You think I've got another boyfriend hidden away somewhere?"

"What am I supposed to think?"

"I'm not two-timing you, Mark."

"You work at the bloody awful pub with guys pawing you and asking you out all the time—"

"Who said that?"

"Lucy."

"Mark, you should check out the customers there. They look like orcs. They go home to Mordor after the pub closes. They don't interest me. Are you jealous?"

"Yes! I admit it! Why wouldn't I be?"

She tries to hold his hand, but he flinches. He gets up and stands, turning his back to her. Behind him the great copper orb of the sun is tangled in tree branches, scattering light across the water. He turns to face her again, but he's cast in silhouette. She has to make a sun visor of her hand in order to see him.

"I don't want to split up with you," he says.

She knows he's telling the truth. "Then don't."

"I really care about you."

Again, she knows he's being sincere.

"But it's not going anywhere, is it?"

"Where is it meant to go? Have you got someone else lined up?"

"No."

That's a lie. It's very clear to her. It flashes at her like a stab of light. Still holding her hand over her eyes to shield her from the brilliant sunlight, she says, "Maybe you should go then."

Mark shakes his head, turns, and begins the long walk across the park. Caz watches him go. He walks alongside the river, across the grass, between the giant cedar trees, and away to the park gates. She watches him all the way.

When he's gone she sinks deep into thought. She's not sure how long she's there before she senses a disturbance. She's not sure which she sees first, the light glimmering from her tattoo or the sparkling light on the river. Caz looks up. What she sees on the water lays a finger of ice on her heart.

It's the woman. She's staring at Caz across the top of her sunglasses. And she's standing in the middle of the river, on the surface of the water, as if it's made of solid glass. She's moving her mouth again without any words coming out. Golden spangles of light scintillate at her feet. Then the sparkling needles of water and light begin to shift and dance, miraculously stitching themselves into words written clearly in threads of gold light: *Accept it.*

Caz gives a tiny laugh, but really it's a little choke of fear. She feels a shocking, cold wave flush over her skin, and for a moment she can't breathe.

She looks around to see if anyone else can see what's happening here, but there's no one else around.

She tries to remember what it was that the old woman told her. *Your other,* she called it. Was this what she meant by her *other*? *Is this thing—this woman, Fizz—my* other? Caz begins to wonder if she comes to tell her when something bad is going to happen, like the guy in the pub assaulting her, or Mark dumping her. Or is it Fizz that is making the bad things happen?

There's one thing she is sure of. And that's that everything has been going wrong, wrong, wrong ever since the curse of the bracelet was passed on to her. She'd had Mark before the incident, and now she's lost him.

Caz sees a stick—a broken tree branch lying by the bench. Grabbing the stick, she runs towards the water and flings it at the ghostly figure of the woman.

The stick hits its target and there's a sudden explosion of white light, the same light that overwhelmed Caz in the church. There is a splash and a sudden flapping of wings. A huge swan explodes out of the light, struggling to fly, finally taking off and soaring just inches above Caz's head.

Caz almost feels the brush of its wings, and the disturbed air current is a wind in her hair as the swan climbs, banks, and turns, flying away towards the sun.

CHAPTER SEVENTEEN

In Case Nothing Goes Wrong

ON MONDAY AFTER school she manages to avoid Mark all day, and in doing so she makes a pretty good job of avoiding Lucy, too. With Lucy she makes the partially true excuse of having to see teachers about the forthcoming exams. Lucy isn't much interested, and Caz suspects her friend is going to fail. She'd help Lucy if she could, but Lucy has too much heavy stuff going on at home. She's still turning up at school lately with a cut on her cheek and a new flashy pair of trainers; or with a split lip and a gold necklace. Bruises and bling.

Dads. Who needs 'em, if that's what they're like?

Caz makes her way alone to the tattoo parlour. She has enough cash for the first session and she's anxious to get on with things. Too much is going wrong in her life. She just hopes the laser treatment won't hurt.

On the way to the shop Caz gets an idea in her head that someone is following her. She turns quickly to see a shadow duck into a shop doorway. She doesn't know if she's just spooking herself. The thought, too, of the laser treatment is creeping her out, but she knows what she's got to do.

When she arrives at the shop, it's open. Caz goes in. The tattooist's electric needle is whining. He is in the middle of a job. A woman who looks about sixty with a bleach-blonde perm and turquoise eye shadow is half-hidden by the tattooist. She's having something fancy done on her back while she sprawls across a bench to read a magazine. Caz can't help but look in the ceiling mirror to see what is going on her back, but there's not much spare skin there at all, in the midst of dragons and red devils and bleeding hearts.

The tattooist looks up at her and turns off his machine. "You ain't eighteen," he sighs. Then he turns his machine back on again.

"Bless her," says the woman receiving the tattoo.

"I came before. About the laser treatment," Caz says boldly.

He stops his machine again and turns back to her. "Oh, yeah. Sit down."

"Bless," says the woman again, flicking through her mag. "I'm just having a name change, duckie, and then he'll be finished with me."

Caz realises that the woman is addressing her. There's a pile of magazines available for customers to read while they wait. Caz picks one up and pretends to be immersed in it. It's called *Biker Chicks*.

"Easier than 'aving it taken off, innit, duckie? Lucky for me it said KEV. I'm 'aving it changed to KEWL, which I know don't mean nuffink but it's better than havin' that prat's name on yer back, innit, duckie?"

Caz looks up from *Biker Chicks* and nods.

Then the woman says, "Like havin' a monkey on yer back, innit?" She finds this hilarious for some reason, and tosses back her head, and cackles.

"Keep still," the tattooist grunts.

"Got a boyfriend, 'ave you, duckie?"

"Not at the moment," says Caz.

"Better off wivout one, ain't that right, Toby?"

"I'm saying nothing," says the tattooist.

"That's 'cos you don't know nuffink. *Har-har!* Ouch! Steady on!"

"Keep still then. Here, I'm just about done."

Toby the tattooist finishes up and switches off his needle pen. He reaches for a mirror and shows the woman his handiwork, like a hairdresser would.

But she turns to Caz. "Has he made a pig's ear of it?"

Caz hasn't much choice but to get up and examine the job. She's not exactly an expert, and anyway the word is pretty much swallowed up amongst all the old partially faded tattoos.

"No," Caz says. "It looks like Kev is history."

"I like that! You hear that, Tobe? Kev is *history*! Like that, I do. *History*." She swings round and pulls her T-shirt back over her head. "What you 'aving done then, girl?"

"I want this removed."

The woman gets up and looks at the tattoo on Caz's wrist. "My life! That's a strange one. Did you put that on, Toby?"

"I don't tattoo kids."

"No, I don't expect you do. But it's unusual, innit? I'd keep that, if I were you."

"You ain't her," says Toby.

"No, I don't expect I am. Well, I'm off." The woman fishes her purse from her handbag and pulls out a couple of notes for Toby. Though he has an electronic till on the premises, Caz notices that the money goes straight in his pocket.

Before the woman leaves, she says to Caz, "Better off wivout a boyfriend, you are." Then she looks at Toby, wrinkles up her nose and squints with her eyes. "Aw, bless!"

When she's gone, Toby the tattooist inserts a little finger in his ear and shakes his head, as if to loosen some wax. Then he sighs. "Come on, let's have you over here."

Before he can do the job, Toby wants Caz to sign some forms releasing him from responsibility if anything goes wrong. Then he knits his brow, suddenly twigging that she would have to be eighteen to legally sign the release forms. He tells her that although she can legally have tattoos removed, the release forms wouldn't be valid, and that she will have to get her parents to sign the release forms.

"No way," says Caz. "Anyway, what can go wrong?"

"Nothing can go wrong. But this is just in case."

Caz once heard Lucy say that if you take your money out and flash it around, most rules can be made to disappear. Caz doesn't really believe this, but she reaches into her pocket and pulls out the money she's earned from The Black Dog. She waves it at Toby.

"How much is the first treatment?"

Toby touches the wax in his ears again. He tosses the release forms aside. "Okay."

Tugging back a curtain at the back of his cluttered property, he reveals a clinical bed with some scary-looking electrical equipment, which Toby proceeds to set up in silence. The machine is about three feet high with a probe on the end. It looks a bit like a dentist's drill with a pen-shaped attachment on the end. Caz can't help feeling like she's in Doctor Frankenstein's laboratory. She gives away her thoughts by wrinkling her nose.

"Never mind how it looks, I'm fully qualified," says Toby. "And what's more, this is an incredibly expensive, high-tech light-pulse laser."

"Do you always know what people are thinking?" Caz says.

"It's all over your face," he says. "Lie down on here and roll your sleeve up. Relax, I'll be a minute or two before I'm ready. I'm going to rub some anaesthetic cream onto your wrist, and when that's taken effect we'll begin."

Toby rubs the cream onto her tattoo. He has a surprisingly gentle touch, though the cream feels cold. While she's waiting for the cream to numb her arm, Caz decides to ask the tattooist about Fizz. "Last time, your girlfriend was here."

"My girlfriend?"

"She looked at my tattoo. Dark-haired. Sunglasses. I think you called her Fizz."

"Fizz?"

"I think so. Where is she?"

"I've no idea what you're talking about, and I've never heard of anyone called Fizz."

"You called her Fizz. I heard it."

"Maybe you heard me say the word 'fizz.' It's what I say when I want to swear. When I've got teenyboppers like you in the shop. Like 'fizz off.' My ex-girlfriend used to tell me I swore too much, so that's why I started saying 'fizz.' Maybe that's what you heard."

Caz looks at him. She somehow knows immediately that he's telling the truth, in the same way that she's coming to know it with everyone. Only this time something else happens. A name pops into her head, and before she knows it, she says it aloud. "Dawn."

Toby looks at her strangely. "What about you? Do you always know what people are thinking, too?"

"Just like you said: it's all over your face."

"What? My girlfriend's name is all over my face? Or ex-girlfriend," he says sadly.

And clearly and from nowhere, in her mind's eye, Caz can see this argument that Toby had with his girlfriend Dawn, in which she's complaining that if only he'd be honest with her, everything would be different. It comes to her in a complete pellet of understanding. She doesn't know how. But she keeps her mouth shut about it. It's too weird.

"Enough talking," he says. "Lie back and keep still." He switches on his machine, which starts up with a low, pulsing hum. He fits special protective glasses over his eyes. "This tattoo of yours, I'm sure it's glowing." He takes the pen attachment and places it over Caz's wrist.

There's a sudden bang and a smell of smoke, and the machine shuts down. Toby rips off his glasses and looks at the machine. Behind him, Caz can see Fizz. She's standing with her hands on her hips. Caz gets a rush of goose bumps all over her body. Fizz takes her sunglasses off and looks Caz in the eye. She shakes her head. Then she's gone.

Toby is already flipping switches on his machine. He takes out the plug and examines the fuse.

"What happened?" asks Caz, looking around the shop for further signs of Fizz. Her face has turned pale and she's shaking.

He doesn't notice. "I think my incredibly expensive, high-tech light-pulse laser just blew up," says Toby.

When Caz gets back home after the failure of the laser, Neville is there. Caz's mum is in the kitchen but he's sitting on the sofa, watching the evening news and eating a cheese sandwich. He puts his sandwich down on his plate when Caz walks in. Caz thinks he looks slightly embarrassed to be back there and eating cheese sandwiches.

"Don't let me interrupt you," Caz says, and she goes up to her room.

She's still thinking about what happened at the tattoo parlour. She'd only seen Fizz very briefly: enough to scare her, but not long enough to guess why she'd been there. Caz was beginning to be afraid of Fizz popping up from behind every parked car and from behind every tree. She dreaded seeing that pale face and sunglasses. She's now certain that she *is* possessed. She seriously wonders if she should tell Neville everything.

But it's so strange she wouldn't know where to begin. Other things are happening. Words are coming out of her mouth that surprise even her. After the machine had blown up and just before she left his studio, Caz had turned to Toby and said, "You should just be honest with Dawn. Tell her everything. She'll have you back, I promise you." These words were out of her mouth before she could stop herself. At first Toby had looked cross. Then he'd looked sad. He'd said nothing: just stared at her. Caz had left without another word. On the way back home she'd looked again at her tattoo. It had faded. It had almost disappeared.

While she's still thinking about whether to confide in Neville, to find out if the church really can help her, there comes a tiny knock on the door.

It's Neville. He's red in the face and his eyes are startlingly wide open.

"I've come to apologise," he says.

"What for?"

"I shouldn't have dragged you down to the church like that. It's not everyone's cup of tea, I know that. Then that business with Elder Collins—it all went too far. I've apologised to your mum and I want to say sorry to you."

"Oh." She's wrong-footed by this. "Forget it."

"Look, Caroline, I'm not very good at these things. Being part of a family, I mean. It's far more complicated than maths. I feel like I'm at the beginning. I tried too hard."

Caz looks at him. He really is embarrassed about it all. She actually feels sorry for him. There's a sweetness behind his awkwardness. He really does need to be accepted by her.

"Can we start again?" he says. "If I get it wrong, you can tell me. Just like I tell you in Maths. Would that work?"

She blinks. "Sure."

"Right then. I'll go downstairs now, shall I?"

Caz nods.

"Okay, I'm off downstairs now." And down the stairs he goes, but with slow, light steps, like he's acting the part of a man who has been sent downstairs after having had a sound telling-off.

Caz closes her bedroom door. She sticks her little finger in her ear and shakes her head. Then she realises it's a trait picked up from Toby the tattooist.

CHAPTER EIGHTEEN
You Missed a Bit

WHEN CAZ NEXT returns to number 13 Briar Street, she once again has the feeling that someone is stalking her. She looks over her shoulder, certain that it must be Fizz. That woman, or spirit or demon or whatever she might be, is haunting her.

There's a summer mist peeling off the river. It muffles the evening's sounds and only adds to the eerie stillness. The footsteps she hears behind her sometimes sound like a dog's paws, sometimes like the patter of rain. Caz senses that if she were to turn suddenly she would catch sight of a hooded shadow moving along a wall or around a corner. Maybe she would even see that dreaded pale face hovering in the air like the moon.

The weather is mild, but these thoughts turn the evening cold.

Caz ducks into a shop doorway herself, to try to catch out whoever is following, but it doesn't work. There's no one there.

"Thought you weren't coming," says Mrs Tranter. "Thought you didn't need to learn no more about it."

"Somehow I'm here," says Caz.

Before letting her in the house, Mrs Tranter looks up the street, as if half-expecting to see someone there. "Come and look at this," says the old woman at last, leading her into the living room.

"What is it?" says Caz.

Mrs Tranter has her arms folded. Her eyes are bright as a bird's, and she nods at a small table with a pecking motion. Caz fails to spot anything unusual. Then it occurs to Caz that Mrs Tranter used to sleep downstairs. "Your bed has gone."

"Not that! I sleep upstairs now that I can move about a bit better. All my health has come back. But that ain't what I'm showing you."

Caz is stumped. She shakes her head.

"Telephone," says Mrs Tranter.

"Oh," says Caz, missing the point.

"Just installed, yesterday. Always wanted one, I did, but could never afford it up until now. But now my luck has changed, ain't it?"

"Maybe."

"No maybe, my girl. You've seen to that. But if you look

you'll see where they've chipped the paintwork off the skirting, putting the wiring in. And they've made a bit of a mess of the wall there. I've got a brush and a pot of paint and I thought you might fix it up while you're here. Shall I fetch it for you?"

Caz sighs as Mrs Tranter goes out and brings back a pot of paint and an old brush. The paint pot looks like it has been around from about the time of World War Two. Together they prise the lid off the pot. The paint inside has gone solid.

"Well, you'll have to go up to the store and fetch me some, then," says the old woman.

Caz blinks at her.

"Well? Are you going to fetch it or ain't you?"

"Give me the money," says Caz. "Before I change my mind."

It takes Caz half an hour to walk to the DIY store, and half an hour to walk back with the new paint. On her return, Mrs Tranter makes her a cup of tea. Caz patches up the woodwork quickly, but the old woman isn't satisfied. She says the new gloss makes the old paint look scruffy, and so Caz will have to paint the skirting board all the way around the room. She stands over Caz, watching her work.

"The other day you started telling me something about a chance," Caz says.

"Chance?"

"Yes! You said something about me waiting for my chance."

Mrs Tranter strokes her chin and looks like she's thinking hard. Caz knows this is all a bit of theatre. Old Tranter knows exactly what Caz is talking about and is merely pretending not to remember. What makes this worse is that the old woman knows perfectly well that Caz has the gift to see through her games. She knows that Caz knows, and is still doing it anyway. Caz would like to flick paint from her brush right in the old woman's eye.

"Oh, yes. Your chance. That's it. Your chance to pass on the curse."

"How do you do that?"

"Well, you have to have a candidate to take it. And they have to reach out for it. That's what I was told, and it was true. You reached out."

"Reach out? I didn't reach out!"

"Oh, yes, you did. You reached out to turn down the corner of the eiderdown, and that was my chance. I took it. And so did you. And you did me a great favour."

Caz closes her eyes for a moment, thinking about that great favour. She resumes the job of painting the skirting board. "There's something I want to ask you," she says. "I've been seeing a woman who no one else can see."

"Oh, yes, that would be your other. Mine was a he. And has she been helping you?"

"Helping me? She's been scaring the liver out of me."

"Yes, they do that. But they also sometimes help. Though you can't always trust them. They're after their own things. They've got their own purposes."

"What purposes? What are they?"

"How do I know? I don't know everything! I was just like you, a silly foolish gal. I had to work it out for myself and *look*!" Mrs Tranter points in horror at the wall, as if something hideous is there. "You've missed that big patch under the chair! I'm not going to tell you these things if you're going to make a bad job of painting."

"I'm not making a bad job!"

"Look at that big patch you've missed! That's a poor job you've made of it! Give me the brush!"

"I'll finish it."

"No, give me the brush and clear off. I'm not telling you anything if you're going to go slack on me."

Caz tries to protest, but old Tranter isn't having any of it. She's down on her ancient knees, and her joints crack as she leans in with vigorous strokes of the brush. For the next few minutes it's almost as if Caz isn't there.

After a while Caz lets herself out of the house. She takes a different route home. She hears a rustle behind her. Now she's certain someone is stalking her.

"Oh, it's you," says Toby the tattooist when Caz appears the following evening. "Do you know how much it cost to fix that machine?"

"Sorry," says Caz. "Not that it was my fault."

"Insurance paid for it," Toby says happily. "And anyway, I'm glad you came in. You ready to go again?"

So they go through the same procedure as before. Toby applies an ointment to the skin around Caz's wrist, to numb it before applying the laser treatment. He's chattering away happily, telling her how he has spoken to his ex-girlfriend Dawn, how he told her everything. Made a clean breast of it. All of it.

All of what? thinks Caz, but she doesn't say anything.

And the amazing thing, Toby tells her, is that they're getting back together. Dawn has brought all her stuff back to the flat. They're even thinking about getting married! How about that!

How about that, Caz thinks.

"Of course, one thing I didn't tell her was that a fifteen-year-old complete stranger told me what to do."

"Fourteen," Caz corrects him.

"Okay. But I still don't know how you did it. In fact I don't think I want to know how you did it. I'm just happy that it worked out." He puts his protective glasses on and switches on the machine. "You ready?"

Toby grips the penlike instrument and directs it towards Caz's tattoo.

There is a short crackle of electricity. The machine has blown up again.

"Don't look at me," Caz says. "I didn't do anything."

Toby doesn't answer. But as he reaches for the switch, uselessly clicking it on then off then on again, all to no avail, he keeps his eyes on Caz.

On the way home from the tattoo parlour, Caz has to pass through a mean part of town. She can take a short-cut across a piece of wasteland and walk down a deserted street where old factory and warehouse buildings stand empty with the wind moaning through all of their poked-out windows, or she can take the long way, which at least has a few passing cars and some streetlights.

Now that she's doubly certain that someone is following her, she really doesn't want to cross the wasteland. She's going to have to go the long way.

She tries to walk a bit faster, remembering the rules: *Don't look weak by walking too fast or too slow; Hold your head up; Look confident; Don't look scared.* As she lifts her head she hears tiny footsteps running up behind her. When she turns, she sees it's only a scrap of newsprint blown along the street. But as she does turn, she catches sight yet again of that figure diving into the shadows. It's someone in a hood.

There's a closed-up pub on the corner. All of its windows are boarded. She turns a street corner and there is a narrow delivery alley, just like there is at The Black Dog. She steps inside it and waits for the person stalking her to pass.

She strains to listen. She can detect the sound of footsteps approaching. The footsteps stop at the corner of the street, as if trying to decide which way to go. Then they scuff at the pavement as they come nearer.

Caz can even recognise the step.

She waits until the last possible moment, and then jumps out on her stalker.

"Now! Why are you following me?"

CHAPTER NINETEEN
See Me in My Office

"SO? WHY ARE YOU following me?" Caz has to repeat her question, because the stalker has fallen backwards in surprise and is rolling around on the pavement. The shock of having Caz jump out like that has knocked him on the ground.

Caz whips back the hood. It's Mark. He's winded himself by falling over. "Give me a break, Caz," he moans.

But Caz is in no mood to give anyone a break. She folds her arms and walks away from the scene, leaving Mark to pull himself to his feet and hobble after her, still clutching his side.

"Slow down, Caz!"

"What do you think you were doing? Spying on me?"

"Slow down, will you? I was worried about you!"

"One day you dump me. Another day you're worried about me. Funny boy."

"I think I cracked a rib."

Finally Caz stops and turns on him. "Why are you wearing a hoodie? It makes you look thick."

"I was worried about you, Caz. Your behaviour is so weird. I think you're in some kind of trouble that you can't tell anyone about."

Caz looks deep into Mark's blue eyes. She doesn't need any special gift to know he's being sincere. "You wouldn't believe me if I told you."

"Try me."

Caz is cross with Mark for following her. But her sense of relief that it is only him is overwhelming. So she spills the lot. Right there. The Creepy. The bracelet. The tattoo. The Black Dog to pay for the laser treatment. Mrs Tranter. It all empties out with a series of thuds like an overturned barrel of apples. She even tells him about Neville and Elder Collins. There's just one thing she holds back: about seeing the truth and the lies.

Mark squints at her in disbelief. He presses his hand to the crown of his head, as if to stop his head from floating off his shoulders. He looks away. He doesn't want to believe all this, but he knows he must.

He asks to inspect the tattoo. "You can hardly see it."

"No. It's strange. It comes and goes. I'm trying to work out *exactly* what makes it do that."

They walk home, slowly, somehow exhausted: Mark by having learned all this, Caz by having unburdened herself.

"I'm behind at school," Caz says. "I'm spending all my time working in the pub or for Mrs Tranter. And when I'm not working, I'm worrying myself sick."

"At least I know you're not seeing someone else. I thought you had another boyfriend."

"I told you I wasn't. Why couldn't you believe me?"

"Sorry, Caz."

"Yeah. Sorry, Caz."

"I'll help you. Anything. What can I do?"

That's just it: what can he do? What can anyone do? Though it helps at least to have someone to whom she can pour it all out.

Mark sees her home. Before leaving her at the gate, he makes to kiss her, but she holds him off.

"Have I blown my chances with you, Caz?"

"I don't know, Mark. I'll see you in school tomorrow, okay?"

Caz lets herself into the house. When she looks out of the window, Mark is gone.

The next day in school, Caz is called to see Mrs Crabb, the Head of Year. Mrs Crabb is a kindly old stick, but she takes no nonsense. She reeks of cigarette smoke because outside of lesson times she is a chain smoker. The fingertips of her right hand are the colour of acorns because of the nicotine, and her teeth look like a mouthful of autumn leaves. Aside from that, the kids like her, and Caz does, too.

She has a "study," which is actually just a stockroom piled high with dusty old books from the 1960s. There's a small desk and two chairs. Even though no smoking is allowed inside the school, Caz thinks the "study" smells like a pub ashtray.

Something's going wrong," says Mrs Crabb, wrinkling her nose and eyeing Caz through the thick glass of her spectacles. "Do you know what it is?"

"No."

"You've not handed homework in lately, and for what work you have done, your marks have slipped. All your teachers have noticed. All of them."

Caz looks away.

"So what's going on?"

"Nothing," says Caz.

"Nothing? It must be a big nothing, Caroline."

Caroline has no answer for her. Mrs Crabb doesn't let her off the hook. She just stares hard. The silence crawls over Caz like a big spider. It's awful. It goes on and on, with Mrs Crabb's eyes magnified behind her spectacles.

Finally Mrs Crabb speaks again. "You're a good student, Caroline. Everyone can see that you're very bright. You've got exams coming up. Don't let it all crash at the last minute like this. It's so important."

"Yes."

"Is everything all right at home?"

"Yes."

"And nothing's worrying you?"

"No." When Caz says this blatant lie she feels a pulse

at her wrist. She can almost feel her tattoo glowing in protest.

"Perhaps you're mixing with the wrong sort of person."

Caz knows that Mrs Crabb means Lucy. She doesn't want to get into a discussion about that.

"You shouldn't let other people drag you down to their level. They'll do that, you know. If they are sinking, they'll try to pull others down, too, just to make themselves feel they haven't been left behind."

Caz suddenly feels protective towards Lucy. "She has a bad time at home. You don't know anything about her."

"I've spoken with her about it. She begged me not to do anything."

Caz is astonished, and a little hurt that Lucy has talked with Mrs Crabb but not with her. "Lucy? Are we talking about Lucy?"

"Of course. Do you think we go around blind? She's very clear about what she wants us to do and not to do. We're monitoring it very closely. I don't know how long we can wait before we have to act. So you don't know everything, do you? And anyway we're here to talk about you, not her."

Caz clamps her lips together.

"Very well," Mrs Crabb says, "I can see I'm not going to get much out of you today. But I want a one hundred percent improvement, okay? And I've got my eye trained on you. All right, you can go."

Caz gets up and reaches for the door handle, relieved to be dismissed at last. But before she does, Mrs Crabb says something that shocks her.

"One more thing. You should do something about your appearance. You were always such a well-turned-out girl. Your hair is a mess. Your clothes are a state. You look like you're letting yourself go."

Caz turns back, stung by these remarks. She could say something very tart about Mrs Crabb's appearance. But she bites her lip.

"Off you go," says Mrs Crabb.

The first thing Caz does is to seek out Lucy. "Do I look a state?"

"What?" says Lucy, puzzled.

"Do I? Do I look a state?"

"What are you talking about?"

"I want to know if you think I look a mess. Crabby just told me that I'm a complete mess."

"She's one to talk! She looks like a bit of black tar left on a cigarette stub!"

"I'm not asking you about Crabby. I'm asking you about me."

Lucy looks away. "You look all right."

A lie. "But has my appearance gone down? You know, since that night. I have to know, Lucy."

Lucy looks at her but says nothing. Which says it all.

"Shit!" says Caz. She storms across the playground, ignoring Lucy, who is calling after her.

Caz bursts into the toilets. Three girls, much younger than her, are in there gossiping. Caz, who never bullies younger kids, screams at them. "Get out!"

They scuttle out quickly. Caz marches up to the mirror. She inspects her skin closely. She drags a hand through her hair.

Then she bursts into tears.

Lucy, having followed her across the playground, bangs open the door. "What's going on?" she demands to know.

"I look like a rat's arse. Look at my hair. Look at my skin. It's this bracelet thing—it's making everything fall apart; it's making *me* fall apart. I just know it."

The toilets door opens again as two more girls try to come in. This time Lucy is the one to yell. *"Get out!"* The door closes quickly.

"It's not the bracelet," says Lucy, "it's the worry. You told me yourself you're not sleeping properly at night. It gets you down. Anyway, you're naturally pretty. Look at me, I have to paint my face whenever we go out. I don't have your looks."

But Caz knows Lucy is just being kind. Contrary to what Crabby says about her dragging people down, she knows Lucy is a real friend. The bell goes for the end of the break.

"Come on," says Lucy. "Dry your eyes. Let's go."

They leave together. Queued up outside of the toilets is a row of nervous-looking girls, all with their legs crossed.

CHAPTER TWENTY
Musical Differences

CAZ CAN'T SLEEP. She's thinks her hair is falling out. She's not sure if she's imagining it or whether there are more strands of hair in her brush than is usual. There are also the spots. Zits, Lucy calls them. Caz has had a fresh outbreak of zits. Her mother has told her that it is normal for someone of her age to have a little acne. *Your hormones,* Helen said.

Could it be that her skin, her hair, her entire body is falling apart? Could it be that her hormones are trying to fight off demons that have taken hold of her? Caz in her pyjamas lies awake, staring up at the dark ceiling. She gets up and fills a glass of water. She pulls the cord on the tiny mirror light and inspects her face in the mirror. She counts her spots. There are seven.

Just as she pulls back from the mirror it seems to her that something moves behind her, reflected in the glass. She half turns, listening hard. If she strains her ears, she can hear the rhythm of her mother's breathing coming from the other bedroom. She shuffles across the landing and touches the door to her mother's room. It moves open a few inches. Caz can see her mother sleeping the sleep of the dead.

Maybe that's what she needs: antidepressant pills that will allow her to sleep. To run away from life.

When she returns to her room, her wardrobe door is hanging open. It seems odd. She knows it wasn't open when she left the room. A wave of goose bumps rushes up her arms. Instinctively she reaches for the light and switches it on.

There's nothing, and no one else, in the room. Caz goes to the wardrobe. Now she can see what pushed the door open: an untidy pile of books and old comics has toppled forward against the wardrobe door from the inside. She stacks the pile of comics more neatly and closes the wardrobe door, turning the key.

Before climbing back in bed she happens to look out of the window. What she sees there lays a finger of ice on her warm beating heat.

It's Fizz.

Surrounded by an eerie grey light, she's in a small silver birch tree that grows between the two neighbouring gardens. Not sitting in the tree. Standing. Standing on a thin twig. Standing on a pencil-thin twig, a branch so flimsy that it would barely support the weight of the smallest wren. She is twenty feet up in the air, balanced on this twig and staring back at Caz. The weird light surrounding her is leaking from behind her dark glasses, like a white gas. She glares back at Caz from behind her smouldering dark glasses, mouthing silent words at her again.

Then she is gone.

No, no, I didn't just see that. I didn't, was Caz's thought. *I'm going mad.*

A voice from behind her forces a choked scream from her throat.

"You're sleepwalking," says Helen. "Come on, let me put you back to bed."

Caz says nothing. She lets her mother steer her back into bed.

But she's not sleepwalking. She's never been more awake in her life. After her mother has gone, she huddles under her duvet, shivering.

On Wednesday night, Caz has to turn out at The Black Dog again. Before going in, she plasters her face with makeup to hide her spots. Lucy has also hit the slap tonight. But she's not hiding spots. The makeup can't completely disguise a small shadow under her eye.

In the bottle room Caz finally can't contain herself. "Why do you put up with it, Lucy? Why?"

It's the first time Caz has ever spoken to Lucy about what happens to her at home. Lucy doesn't blink, or stop what she's doing for a second. "Where would I go? What would I do?"

And Caz can't answer that.

"There was a girl in school who went to her teachers about the same thing. They investigated it, got the police involved, everything. The girl was taken away and placed in a care home. A government care home. I wonder if she ever went up to her teachers and said, 'Thanks a fucking bunch.'"

Caz blinks at her. There is no answer, it seems. The subject is closed as soon as it is opened.

It's a strange night at the pub. The band playing that evening are spectacularly bad—so awful that people drift away—and by ten o'clock only a handful of drinkers are left. They sound less like a rock band than a group of road diggers in hard helmets.

Caz hears Frank swear. "That's it!" he shouts above the industrial din. He marches to the side of the stage and suddenly the guitars go dead. The drummer plays on regardless. He's in his own world, drumming with his eyes closed. The singer, a guy with eyebrows that join in the middle and a ratty fringe hanging in his eyes, bellows away for a few moments until he catches the sound of his own miserable wailing. He looks astonished at how bad his voice is, as if he's never heard it before. Then the drummer opens his eyes and drops one of his drumsticks.

The band all turn and look at each other. Then they all

look at Frank. He's holding the main supply plug high up in the air for them to see. The entire pub goes quiet, as do Caz, Lucy, and the rest of the bar staff. The silence is broken by someone who claps and cheers Frank's intervention.

"You'll thank me for this one day," Frank says.

"What?" spits the singer.

"Every young band needs to be told the truth of how bad they are if they're to get better. That's why I say you'll thank me when I tell you that you are the biggest pile of garbage ever to stand on that stage. And believe me we've had some crap here at The Black Dog."

"I'll second that!" shouts one of the stalwart drinkers.

"So I'm helping your career when I say you've got five minutes to get your gear out of my pub. All of it. If it's not gone in five minutes, I will set fire to it and throw it in the canal."

"You'll have to come past the four of us first," sneers the singer.

Frank is so fast Caz is astonished. He jumps onstage and grabs the young vocalist by the collar and the back of his jeans and carries him outside. The door opens and closes behind him. In a second Frank, is back. "Who's next?" he says.

"We're goin'," says the drummer, already unscrewing his cymbals.

"Good boy. Good luck with your next gig." Frank turns to Liz behind the bar. "Now then, give my loyal customers—all four of them—a free drink."

Within the allotted five minutes the band has gone, and

their gear with them. Frank switches on the jukebox at the back of the pub and selects some really old shit. It's the kind of stuff Caz's mother would listen to. Maybe even older. Frank takes a bottle of scotch whisky and retires to a table in the corner. He pours himself a large glass and whips out a paperback book, like he's switched off for the night.

"Oooch," Liz whispers to the girls. "Roy Orbison. When he listens to Roy Orbison don't go anywhere near him."

"Right," says Caz. "Right."

With almost no customers, there are few glasses to collect and wash. Lucy and Caz clean the ashtrays and wipe down the empty tables, but there is little more for them to do. They wonder if they should go home, but they daren't ask Frank, hooded and cowled in a mood so black it seems to radiate from his chosen corner. The sweet Roy Orbison vocals do nothing to cheer up the mood of the pub. The diehards who stayed behind drink quietly and even two of them get up to leave without a word.

Half an hour before closing time Caz says, "I'm going over."

"Over where?" says Lucy.

She nods towards Frank.

"You're mad! Keep away from him tonight."

But Caz ignores her. She goes to his table, carefully draws back a chair, and sits down. She says nothing.

Frank ignores her. He just reads his book—very rapidly, and when he turns the pages it is with alarming force.

It's an incredible ten minutes before Frank even acknowledges her presence. He does this by lowering the paperback a fraction and looking at her across the top of the book. Caz simply folds her hands on her lap. Frank goes back to reading.

After a few more minutes he lays the book on the table and looks at her hard.

She says nothing. She's conscious of clinking glasses and the tidying motions of the bar staff behind her. She knows that everyone is observing but without daring to look at them directly.

"What?" says Frank.

"I didn't say anything," says Caz.

"That's a lie."

"No, it's not. I didn't say anything."

"You think? A man spins some Roy Orbison on the jukebox. He goes to a corner of the room with his whisky bottle. He sticks his nose in a book. He's saying to the whole world: *Sod off and die.* But you walk across the room and sit next to him. What's that saying?"

"You're right. I'm just saying: *She'd be the same age as me.*"

Frank stiffens. He stiffens *visibly.* He looks up and all round the pub at his staff.

"No," Caz says, "no one told me. I don't think anyone here knows, do they? It's just me. I don't even know how or why. But I see some things. I see things and I know things."

Frank squints at her. He wrinkles his nose and scratches it as if he has a sudden itch. "Are you completely insane?"

"I might be going that way. I don't know why it is. I'm

upset all the time these days. But I thought you might talk to me. Because I'm the same age she would have been. Almost exactly."

Frank looks at her with angry eyes. "How old are you?"

Caz tells him. "I think she would have been perhaps two months older than me."

"How the fuck do you know this?"

"I don't know, Frank. I just look at people and I know things."

"Oh? And are you going to tell me that she's happy where she is? That she wants me to know everything is all right? Are you going to tell me all that crap? 'Cos I've had all that. I went to psychics and mediums all over the place. I've heard the best. And it's all rubbish. Complete rot."

"No. I'm not telling you any of that. Because what I see is not about her. It's about you."

Frank is about to reply when the jukebox stops, having reached the end of its cycle. He stands up. *"I want Roy! Will somebody put more Roy on! And turn up the bloody volume."*

He sits down again. Caz hears a scuttling behind her. Somebody cranks up the jukebox again with more of Frank's favourite music, but louder, stirring, echoing round the pub.

"Just who the hell are you?" says Frank.

She knows he means it nastily but she smiles and holds out her hand. "I'm Caz."

He snorts. Shakes his head in disbelief. Ignoring her offered handshake, he says, "Well, what do you know, Caz?"

"I know it wasn't your fault. There was nothing that could be blamed on you. She was three years old and it could have happened to anyone. But you've never stopped punishing yourself these last eleven years. Drinking so you don't have to feel it. Bit like my mum. But with pills. I don't understand any of this. I'm only fourteen. But this is what I see." And she places her hand on his leathery, tanned wrist.

Frank looks at her pale hand aghast. And his eyes begin to well with water. With his favourite music reverberating round the almost empty pub, this scary man just looks at Caz's hand on his, and the tears pour down his face.

Afterwards Lucy gets cross with Caz when she won't tell her what she and Frank were talking about.

"It's personal," says Caz.

"Fine," says Lucy in that way that means "not fine." She folds her arms and looks out of the taxicab window.

Caz looks out of the window on her side of the cab. Not that she sees anything: she's too busy thinking about how it happened—how she knows what she does about Frank, how she knew how to walk over to him.

Because she'd seen it all. She'd seen that Frank, hard-man hard-hearted hard-boozer, used to be a schoolteacher. Yes, incredible. A teacher, just like Neville, she supposes, or maybe not quite like Neville, but not much different from all the other male teachers in the school. And he had a wife and a daughter—Caz even knew the name of the daughter—*Jennie*—though not the name of the wife. And the daughter Jennie had died when she fell out of a window. Frank who had left the window open had never forgiven himself. His wife had left him and he turned to drink to soak away his guilt and anger and shame, never talking about it, never referring to the little girl by name.

Of course it is astonishing that Caz can see all that without anyone ever telling her. Amazing and uncanny and weird. But that isn't what she is thinking about as the taxi drives through the town to take the girls back to their homes.

Caz is thinking about this curse, the curse of the bracelet that has left her with this gift to see things, to see into people.

In the back of the cab, with the amber-coloured streetlamps and the green traffic lights sweeping across the passenger seats, she looks down at the tattoo on her wrist. It is so faint it has almost disappeared.

For the first time Caz sees that this curse might actually be a way of helping people.

CHAPTER TWENTY-ONE
Beware the Pineapple Slice

"BY PUTTING THE BRACELET on somebody else? Is that the only way I can get rid of it?" Caz is back at Mrs Tranter's house. She's painting again. The old slave-driver has decided that after freshening up the woodwork with a coat of gloss, the walls are now looking a little grubby. So she has Caz sloshing emulsion on the walls with a paint roller.

"Yes. But it ain't easy." Mrs Tranter pours a little of her tea into her saucer and drinks from the saucer with that disgusting slurping noise. "They have to reach out for it, at the right time. I waited fifty years for you."

Caz stops painting. "Fifty years! Fifty!"

"That's right. Work while you talk, gal; work while you talk. And make sure you don't splash my new furniture."

Mrs Tranter has had a new sofa delivered. Though the

paint can't harm it, because it still has its plastic wrappings. Everything is perking up for Mrs Tranter since she passed on the bracelet to Caz. She's started applying eye shadow and makeup, which Caz thinks makes her look like Judy from a Punch theatre at the seaside. She's also bought herself a TV set and a new coat. She shows Caz the new coat and puts it on.

"I'm off for my three o'clock," she says.

"Three o'clock what?" says Caz, stopping her brushwork.

"I always have a three o'clock on a Saturday. Even if it's only to feed the ducks in the park. Today I'm going to have my fortune told, since everything is looking brighter. But you needn't stop working. I'll be back in a while."

Then she's gone, leaving Caz to her work. Caz feels like walking out but she still has so many things she wants to ask. It's over an hour and a half before Mrs Tranter returns, proclaiming that she's been told to look forward to "a bright future."

Caz isn't interested in the future. She wants to talk about *right now.* "There's another thing: I don't even have the bracelet."

"No. You have to find it."

"Where?"

"Where? How do I know where? You must look for it. Where did you leave it?"

"I didn't leave it. It just fell off when I was sleeping and I never saw it again."

"Well, you must look where it fell off."

The temptation to flick paint at Mrs Tranter, still in her new coat, isn't going away. But Caz resists. "I've got another question for you. Have you ever used it to do good?"

"Good? What good could it do?"

Caz is astonished. It's obviously never occurred to the old woman that the curse might be used in this way. Not a curse but a gift. Fifty years, and she's never seen a way to help people with it. Caz puts down her paint roller and strips off the old sweatshirt she's been wearing.

"Where you going?" shrieks Mrs Tranter.

"That's enough for today."

"You 'aven't finished! You finish when I say you do and not before!"

"No, I don't. I'll be back another day."

Caz lets herself out, ignoring the shrieks and protests filling the hall behind her.

Back home, Neville is having supper with them. They are having gammon. Caz's mum has put a slice of pineapple on top of the gammon. Caz notices these odd little changes that appear whenever Neville is around. Pineapple slice: Neville. No pineapple slice: no Neville.

"Is Mark Morris a friend of yours?" Neville says brightly.

Caz nearly chokes on her piece of pineapple. She looks up warily. "Yes."

"He was in church on Sunday."

"What?"

"Yes."

"What, your church?"

"Yes."

"You mean he was at your weird evangelical shake-it-all-about church?"

"Caroline!" says Helen.

Neville laughs. "It's all right. Yes. My shake-it-all-about church. He was there on Sunday. With a friend. He was very interested. Showed a lot of interest in joining the youth club, too. Wanted to meet Elder Collins. Said he'd heard a lot of good things about him."

"Not from me he didn't!" splutters Caz.

"No, I dare say he'd picked it up from someone else. He's a decent lad, though, Mark. Very decent."

Caz saws thoughtfully on her gammon joint, wondering, *What's Mark up to?* The rest of the meal passes quietly.

Later that evening, Helen pops out to the shops. Neville is sitting at the front room table marking a huge pile of exercise books. It seems odd to Caz to think of her schoolteachers having their own lives out of the classroom. Maybe she used to think that teachers had a switch at the back of their heads that clicked off at home time, and that they were stacked upright in the school staff room overnight until they were required again the next day. Caz watches him working quickly through the pile of books, tutting, muttering, writing comments at the foot of the page.

"Is it hard being a teacher?" Caz asks.

Neville doesn't stop working. "Well, it's not easy."

"Do you like it?"

"I like to think I'm helping people by teaching."

"Not everyone wants to be helped."

He smiles but continues to mark the work. "That's right. And for those, I do wonder what the hell I'm supposed to do. But you do it anyway."

Caz leaves him to his marking, but after a while, without looking up, he says, "Am I forgiven?"

"What for?"

"Oh, that episode at the shake-it-all-about."

"Yes."

"I've discovered there's a lot more to you than meets the eye, Caroline."

"Oh?"

He stops marking for the first time and turns to face her. He points his red pen at her. "I know that you go helping old ladies, for example. Tidying and painting."

"Have you been following me?"

"Not me. Mark told me about you."

"I'll kill him!"

"Don't be mad with Mark. He was worried about what you were doing. He and I get along pretty well. Anyway, he told me about your voluntary work. I think it's brilliant."

If only you knew, thinks Caz.

But Neville has other fish to fry. "I'm very fond of your mum, you know."

"Uh."

"And though she's not quite as fond of me as I am of her, I think she could get to like me even better."

"She likes you well enough," Caz hears herself saying.

"But one day I hope she'll want to take it further."

"What do you mean by 'further'?"

Neville looks a little shy. He raises his eyebrows at her. They don't come down.

It dawns on Caz what he means. "You want to marry her?"

His eyebrows still don't come down. "Is it a really stupid and terrible idea? You can be honest."

"Heck, I don't know what to say to that!" She really doesn't. She's stumped for words. "Heck."

"I just thought I'd be honest with you. I hope you don't mind. I'm trying to remember that though you're in my class at school, I don't have to treat you that way when we're out of school."

"No, that's fine."

"I'm telling you what's on my mind. But I'd like to trust you not to say anything about it to your mum. Not just yet."

"Okay, I won't."

Neville smiles. "Funny. I feel a lot better now I've told you that. A whole lot better."

Caz excuses herself. She says she needs a drink of water.

The next day Caz makes yet another visit to Toby's tattoo parlour. She is accumulating money from her glass-collecting job and so far hasn't spent a penny of it. Toby is glad to see her, despite what happened to his expensive equipment. He chatters away to her and reassures her that the equipment has been repaired. He has, he says, used it on three different customers since Caz was here last and that all the technical problems have been fixed.

While he swabs her skin with the anaesthetic, he cheerfully prattles on about how well he and his girlfriend are getting along. Then he stuns Caz by asking her, quite seriously, "Do you think I should ask her to marry me?"

Caz blinks at him. "How can I answer that? I'm only fourteen! What do I know about it?"

Toby stops swabbing and then thinks about it. "Yes. I suppose you're right."

"I mean, if I'm not old enough to get a tattoo then I'm not old enough to advise you about marriage." *Why are all these older people asking my advice about marriage?* she wonders. *I'm like an agony aunt.*

"No. Quite right. You're not. Don't know what I was thinking of. Do you know something? I can barely see this tattoo."

Caz looks. It's true. It's quite faint, but it's still there. And only she knows that its bright colours come and go. "Go ahead anyway."

Toby throws a switch on his machine and the familiar humming commences. He takes hold of the pen, but before he applies it to her skin he says, "But I'd just like to know your opinion. Do you think I should wait awhile? Or should I ask her while everything is going great?"

"Toby!"

"Yeah. You're right. You're just a kid. What would you know?"

He sighs and applies the light beam to Caz's wrist.

There's a crackle and a puff of smoke as the machine blows up again.

Caz's heart sinks. Toby holds his head in his hands for a very long time.

CHAPTER TWENTY-TWO
Not Just Any Old Boyfriend

THE NEXT FEW DAYS at school are difficult for Caz. Mark is distant and Lucy won't talk to her. Whenever she approaches her friend, Lucy just disses her and walks away. What's worse is that sometimes she sees Mark and Lucy together, whispering. She knows they are talking about her.

Caz decides to have it out with Lucy. She waits for a break time and she stalks Lucy, knowing that she'll need to use the girls' toilets at some time. Sure enough, just before the end of break, Lucy goes into the girls' toilets. Caz follows her and waits outside one of the stalls. A few younger girls are giggling and gossiping by the washbasins. When Caz hears Lucy flush the toilet she turns to the younger girls. "Right, you lot! Out! Now!"

The girls obey meekly.

Lucy comes out of the stall but Caz, with arms folded, bars her way. Lucy tries to slip by but Caz takes a step to the right to stop her. Lucy moves the other way, but Caz steps left, blocking her again.

"Get out of my way," Lucy says.

Caz shakes her head.

Lucy's dark brown eyes look angry. "Do you want me to push you out of the way?"

Before Caz can answer, the bell sounds to signal the start of the next lesson. The girls stare each other out. Lucy blinks first. "I have to get to my class."

"You've never been in a hurry to get to class before."

"Well, I am now. And if you don't step aside, I'll slap you."

Caz sees that Lucy means it. "Yeah, that's your dad's answer to everything, isn't it? If it gets in his way, he slaps it."

Lucy raises her fist to hit Caz, but Caz doesn't flinch. "Go ahead. That's what he would do, isn't it? And I'm your best friend. Why not hit your best friend?"

"Don't you talk about my dad. You know nothing about it!"

"But I do, Lucy. I know the things you've never told me. I know that your earliest memory of being slapped is when you were three, maybe four. Your dad was lying on the sofa drinking beer from a can, watching the football on telly. You ran to give him a hug and to show him your dolly. And he just lashed out at you with the back of his hand. For no reason. Just to shut you up. Just to get you out of the way. You ran away, crying your eyes out. And then after he'd slept off his drink, he went out and bought you a big fluffy toy dog with a blue collar. You've still got that dog. I've seen it in your room."

Lucy shakes her head in disbelief. "How do you know all of this?"

"I can see it all, Lucy. I've been watching it in you recently. Every beating. Every single stupid makeup gift."

Lucy suddenly bursts into tears. Huge years-old sobs that seem to be drawn up from deep in her belly. Caz is about to comfort her when the door bursts open. It's Mrs Crabb, Head of Year, reeking of cigarettes as usual. "Girls! What are you doing here? Get to your lessons at once!" Then she spots that Lucy is sobbing. "Lucy, whatever is it?"

"It's all right, Lucy, I'll explain," says Caz. "Mrs Crabb, this is something that Lucy and I can't tell you about right now. But even though it's lesson time, I need to talk to Lucy. So I'm asking for permission to take a few minutes off our next lesson."

"Not unless you tell me what the matter is! Of course not!"

"I'm sorry. It's not something you can help us with. Except by allowing us to talk."

Mrs Crabb looks hard at Caz through her thick glass spectacles, then strokes her chin with nicotine-stained fingers. Behind her glasses her eyes float like tadpoles in a pond as she decides what to do. "All right," she says at last. "Come with me."

She leads the girls to her stockroom-office. Unlocking the door for them, she ushers them inside. "Sit down. I'll be back in twenty minutes. Make those twenty minutes count." Then she closes the door, leaving the girls to it.

"This is like sitting in an old ashtray. Have you got power over Mrs Crabb, too?" Lucy wants to know. She's stopped crying and has set her face hard again.

"Don't talk rubbish. I haven't got any power over anyone."

"How do you know all this stuff, Caz? How?"

"I don't know! It's something to do with the bracelet. I can just see people's stories inside them. I can see what hurts them or what upsets them, or why they are like they are. I don't know why it is. And I can't see everything. I can't see why you're being so iffy with me."

"It's you, Caz. You've been distant. I don't know where you are. You won't tell me anything. I don't know where you go. You wouldn't even tell me what you were talking about to Frank at the pub the other night."

"I can't. It's about *his* story. It's too private."

Lucy looks away. So Caz fills her in on everything she can. She tells her about how she's been going to the old woman's house. Lucy is astonished. She recounts the saga of the laser machine at Toby's tattoo parlour and the business about it blowing up every time she tries to get treatment. She explains about Mark and how everything has gone wrong. "So I've had my own problems to worry about. In fact I'm so worried about all this stuff that every time I wake up in the morning, I feel like throwing up."

"I'm sorry," Lucy says. "Not much of a friend, am I?"

"You are, Lucy. You are. And what are we gonna do about this thing with you and your dad? It's getting worse, isn't it?"

Lucy nods. She rolls up her sleeve and shows Caz some fresh bruises near the top of her arm.

"You don't have to put up with it, you know."

"Caz! Like I've said before: where else am I going to go? Go out on the streets and sell my body to old guys who like schoolgirls?"

"I'm going to ask my mum if you can move in with us."

"Get real, Caz. Your mum can only just manage to support the two of you on what she earns."

"We could chip in. We're earning money ourselves now. It could work."

Lucy starts crying again. "Why are you so good to me when I'm always shitty to you?"

"You're not, Lucy, you're not. Come on, get yourself together. Crabby will be back soon. Look, we'll help each other out, right? You help me with this tattoo and I'll help you with your dad. That's what friends are for."

Caz leans over and pinches Lucy's cheek between her thumb and forefinger, and waggles it. It makes Lucy laugh.

Pretty soon there comes a gentle knock on the door and Mrs Crabb opens it. "Are we done?"

The girls both stand up.

"Is there anything I can help with?"

"No, we're all right," says Caz.

"And you, Lucy?"

"I'm all right."

"Are you sure?"

"Well," Lucy says, "this room smells a bit rough, miss."

That night Caz puts it to her mother. "Can Lucy live here with us?"

"What? You must be joking. It's bad enough having you around like a wet weekend."

"I'm not joking, Mum. Her dad beats the crap out of her."

"Are you serious?"

Caz nods.

Helen wrinkles her brow. She gets up and goes into the kitchen. Caz follows her in. Helen, as she always does when troubled, snatches up a damp cleaning cloth and starts gruelling away at the kitchen work surfaces. "It's a big thing you're asking. What would her parents say? And if she's being knocked about, it's a matter for the police."

"It's not that easy. She wouldn't want to involve the police. And I doubt if they really care enough about her to mind if she came here. And I've thought about the money," says Caz. "We're both earning from our job at the pub."

"Pub? I thought you worked in a wine bar?"

"Wine bar, I mean. We could help with the housekeeping."

Helen starts in on the sink drainer, sprinkling bleach ahead of her cloth. "Plus I'm not sure she's a good influence on you. Do you think I haven't noticed that tattoo you've been hiding from me?"

Caz is floored. She wants to protest that Lucy had nothing to do with her getting the tattoo, but, of course, she did.

Helen sees Caz's face crash at the revelation that her mum has known about the tattoo all along. "For goodness' sake, Caroline, I'm not cross about the tattoo. I'm more disappointed that you didn't want to talk about it with me before getting the thing done. I feel like I'm losing you as a friend. Come here. Let me look." Helen takes Caz's wrist and inspects the markings there. "It's so faint you can hardly see it anyway."

"You're not losing me, Mum."

Helen lets Caz's wrist fall. "So you two have talked about this?"

"About the tattoo?"

"No! I don't care about the tattoo! I mean about Lucy moving in."

Caz has to recover. Then she says, "Lucy doesn't think it's possible. But I know she wants to get away. I know it."

Helen blinks at her. Caz can almost see the cogs turning in her mum's brain. She can also see that there is something her mother is not telling her. It's connected with Neville.

"I'll think about it," Helen says.

It's more than Caz could have hoped for.

The next day at school she tells Lucy it might just be possible. She wants to know what Lucy's parents would make of the idea. Lucy shrugs and said if she decided to do it then her parents would go along with it. Caz was right: they don't really care enough one way or the other. Caz puts it to Lucy that if she can swing it with her mum that Lucy would come and live with them. Lucy agrees. She tries to act casual about the idea, but Caz can see that there is a hurt little girl inside Lucy who desperately wants it to happen.

"If I can persuade her," Caz says, "and it's a big *if* . . ."

"Yeah?"

"If I can swing it, there is something you need to know."

"Yeah?"

"I mean, if you *did* come to live with us, you'd really need to know this about us."

"Yeah?"

"Well . . ."

"For God's sake, Caz!"

"It's like this: Mum has a boyfriend."

"So what? I wouldn't have to shag him, would I?" Lucy sees Caz wince at the picture of that idea. "Just kidding!"

"No, you wouldn't have to do anything like that. It's just who he is."

"Yeah? So what's the big deal?"

"It's Neville Corkhill."

"What?"

CHAPTER TWENTY-THREE
Hold Out Your Hand

ON FRIDAY NIGHT at The Black Dog, Frank doesn't speak to Caz or Lucy for the first two hours. He doesn't even make eye contact. Caz frets that he is angry with her over the night she tried to help him. Then, halfway through the evening, he calls Caz and Lucy into the bottle room. Caz tells Lucy that they're both about to get fired.

But Caz is wrong. Frank has a gift for each of them. The gifts are prettily wrapped. They open them. It's a shiny MP3 player apiece.

Lucy looks puzzled but happy. "Wow, this is great! What's it for?"

"A bonus," Frank says gruffly.

"Bonus! Yay!" Lucy bounds over to him and mashes her lips against his unshaven cheek.

"Don't slobber all over me. And don't tell the other staff. Please."

Caz looks hard at Frank, who still doesn't seem to want to meet her eye. "This is lovely, Frank," she says quietly. "Thank you."

"I was wondering," Frank says, "if there's somewhere you wanted me to take you."

"Come again?" says Lucy.

"I mean, if you need a ride somewhere. If you want to go out one night—both of you, of course. I could drive you. Drop you off and pick you up later. Stuff like that."

The girls are dumbstruck, staring at him.

"Anyway, think about it." Then Frank claps his big leathery hands explosively. "And now you idle little vixens, you can *get back to work* because there are *glasses piling up out there! Right!*"

The girls scuttle back to work. In the hubbub of the bar, Lucy has to shout to Caz to make herself heard. "What's going on? Is he trying to get in our pants?"

"No," Caz shouts back with a smile. "He's not. I'll explain later."

Caz saw *everything* when Frank gave them the MP3 players. She understands exactly what's going on in his head. She'll have to find a way to explain to Lucy that Frank knows firstly that Caz's father left home, and secondly that Caz has hinted to him that Lucy's old man knocks her about. After what happened the other night, when Frank grasped the idea that both girls are about the same age as his own daughter would have been, he's trying to find a way of being "Dad."

Frank is not in the habit of buying extra gifts for his staff. He's seeing what it's like to be a good dad to a pair of fourteen-year-old girls. That's why he offered to be a taxi service to them. He's been careful to include Lucy, so that no one would get the wrong idea about his intentions.

Caz read *all* of this in his face when he handed over the gifts. Her power to know things about people is getting stronger all the time. It shocks her sometimes. She doesn't know whether to feel proud or terrified. The truth is she feels both.

She could tell Frank that it doesn't matter; he doesn't have to try so hard. But she knows he desperately wants to change the way he is. She knows that she and Lucy can help him.

It's a weird evening. After giving them the MP3s, Frank steers clear of them again. Even when it's time for them to go home, he barely has much to say. He's sitting with his bar staff as usual when the girls' cab arrives. But tonight he gets up and walks them to the cab and holds the door open for them. That's it. No words, no good-night. Lucy makes big round eyes at Caz.

The night is mild, so instead of going straight home they get the cabbie to drop them off near the river. From there they walk across the park to the bandstand. Caz explains what she knows. She has to tell Lucy just a little of the personal tragedy in Frank's life.

"That's so sad," Lucy says.

"It explains the way he behaves," says Caz.

"Why he drinks so much. Why he's so mean."

"But we mustn't take advantage of it."

"You mean we have to give the MP3s back?"

"No. But we shouldn't let him keep buying us stuff."

"Well, at least it means he's not trying to shag us."

"Yes, that's a relief."

"Shame," says Lucy, laughing.

"You slut! You don't mean that."

"No, I was joking."

Caz looks at her friend. She can see that Lucy is joking, and then again she isn't. Not completely.

"Slut," Caz says again.

On Saturday, Caz returns to Mrs Tranter's house. The old woman is in a vile mood. She's ordered a dishwasher but it seems there has been some problem with the plumbing. A pipe has leaked and the kitchen got flooded.

"What's so funny about that?" says Mrs Tranter when she sees Caz trying to suppress a little smile.

"Nothing."

"What you grinning for, then?"

"I'm not." But she is grinning. The truth is Caz can't help feeling just a tiny bit gleeful on hearing that not absolutely everything is on the up-and-up for Mrs Tranter; it might mean that not absolutely everything is on the slide for Caz. "What do you want me to do today?"

"Upstairs. I'm sorting out my new bedroom."

Caz follows the old woman upstairs. The wooden banister rail creaks, just as it did that night. She remembers very clearly that she and Lucy went upstairs in the dark before coming back down again on the night the bracelet was clamped on her wrist. It brings the moment back to her. It makes her more than a little afraid.

Although Mrs Tranter has moved her bedroom upstairs, it is laid it out in almost the same way as her original bedroom. She has even brought upstairs the same heavy flower-patterned curtains to hang at the windows, with dusty old net curtains behind them. There is the same odour of dead flowers. On the same bedside table is the old-fashioned alarm with roman numerals and twin bells perching at the top of the clock. Caz remembers looking at it the night she did the Creepy, before the hall clock struck one and her life was changed.

Mrs Tranter seems to have no idea about what significance seeing this bedroom might have for Caz. "I want this room to have a complete makeover," she says. "I want you to start by lifting down them curtains. Here, you'll need to stand on a chair."

Caz does as she's asked. The curtains are dusty. The net curtains behind it are so dry and brittle they almost break at the touch.

Caz knows she's getting near to the end of what Mrs Tranter can tell her about the bracelet and its powers. She senses that the old woman is becoming evasive. They both know that when there's nothing left to tell, then the old woman will no longer be able to use Caz as a source of free labour. But she's determined to pump her for whatever information she can.

"I want you to tell me," Caz says, "about the person who gave you the bracelet."

"I don't know much about her," Mrs Tranter says. "She

tricked me into holding my hand out for payment for a little job I'd done her. But don't get ideas, because it won't work with me. I've got all my marbles, I have, and you won't find me so dumb a second time."

"Who was she?"

"I've told you: I know nothing about her. She was a gypsy with a painted caravan pulled by a big grey horse. She walked her horse and caravan onto a piece of wasteland behind where I lived, and as she spied me watching her, she asked me to fetch her a mug of tea. Well, I didn't like gypsies, and I didn't like being ordered about like that, so I fetched her a mug of tea all right, but I put some salt in it. She drank the tea and called me back, and said she would reward me for the tea. I held out my hand for my reward and she clamped the bracelet on me. Then she went on her way. Of course I didn't know what she'd paid me with until much later."

"I wonder who had given it to her?" Caz thinks of a long line of women passing on the bracelet, back into the mists of time.

"I've given up wondering about that. Now stop your prattle and let's give these windows a clean."

Caz washes the window before hanging the new curtains. The water in her bucket turns black. She pumps Mrs Tranter for more information. There's nothing she can offer Caz that she hasn't told her already. When Caz finishes hanging the new curtains, she steps down and surveys her work.

"Now I want you to wipe down the woodwork so I can have it painted."

Caz knows that she means so that Caz can paint it. But Caz is done. "Nope. I'm finished."

"Finished? You've only just got here."

"I've been here two hours," Caz says pointing at the clock. "That said ten o'clock when I got here."

"You're a lazy gal, that's for sure. Well, you can at least wind up my clock for me before you go."

Caz shakes her head. Mrs Tranter is the kind of person who will squeeze every tiny drop of work out of her if she can. Even down to the winding of a clock. Caz picks up the old alarm clock and winds it anyway. As she winds the clock, she notices that the alarm is set for seven in the morning. She imagines Mrs Tranter reaching out her bony hand to switch off the alarm at seven o'clock every morning for fifty years. Carefully replacing the clock on the bedside table, she makes her way downstairs. Mrs Tranter follows.

Caz sees that a couple of letters have arrived while she's been working, so she picks them up from the doormat. "Here's your post," she says, handing them to Mrs Tranter.

Mrs Tranter folds her arms. "Leave them on the table."

"Take them," says Caz.

Their eyes meet. Mrs Tranter's yellow eyes, like those of a cunning bird of prey, and Caz's clear, strong blue eyes. They both know that Caz is testing the old woman, seeing if she will reach out to accept the letters. The old woman has no way of knowing whether Caz has found the bracelet, and even if she has, she's not going to get caught again. They don't have to speak. Their eyes say all of this to each other.

Caz smiles and lays the letters down on the table. "I don't think I'll be back again, Mrs Tranter."

"You'll be back," says the old woman.

"I don't think so." Caz closes the door behind her.

Sunday is even odder. Neville appears in the late afternoon with reports that he's seen Mark at church again. And this time Mark had brought with him Conrad and another boy from school. Neville describes Mark as "a great recruiter."

"At this rate we'll have half the school there," says Neville cheerfully. "Which would be terrific."

Don't count on it, thinks Caz. But she knows she's really going to have to have a word with Mark.

When Helen goes upstairs, Caz changes the subject. "Do you think," she asks Neville, "that you could persuade Mum to stop taking the antidepressant tablets?"

Neville looks astonished, as if Caz has somehow been reading his mind. He extends his hand, looking to shake on it. "That's amazing! I was just thinking the very same thing!"

Caz shakes his hand. "We'll work on her together."

Caz goes to bed content in the knowledge that she and Neville are planning to wean Helen off the pills. They both think she will be so much better off without them. She's seen how Neville can be an ally, someone willing to help. She's already softening in her attitude towards him.

Later, just as Caz is falling asleep, she's disturbed by a slithering sound. Then her wardrobe door flies open, followed by the sound of objects bumping on the floor. She sits up in bed.

Caz flicks on her bedside light. She stares at the wardrobe door hanging open. All that's happened is that the same pile of books and comics from the wardrobe floor has slipped forward again and pushed the door open.

Caz sighs. Clutching at her heart, which is still thudding inside her ribs, she gets out of bed and piles the books and comics back inside the wardrobe. She closes the door on the unsteady pile and turns the key.

Then she climbs back in bed and lies on her side, staring at the wardrobe door until she finally falls asleep.

CHAPTER TWENTY-FOUR

The Great Only Appear Great Because We Are on Our Knees!

CAZ THINKS SHE knows how she might get rid of the bracelet . . . if only she can find the thing. No matter how many times she searches her bedroom or the rest of the house, there is no sign of it. She has emptied drawers and turned out cupboards to see if her mother might have found it and put it away somewhere. It never shows up.

Plus she has other things to think about. Like her schoolwork. Caz is not dumb: she knows she can't afford to let it slip. She has plans and she wants to get good grades. She's also still terrified about her appearance. She keeps checking the loose hair in her brushes, and examining herself for spots in the mirror. She also inspects the tattoo: today it is dull.

There's another thing. She wants to know what Mark

is up to. She seeks him out by the bike sheds at lunchtime. He's larking around with Conrad and another couple of lads. "Conrad, can you leave me and Mark to have a chat?" she says loudly.

The boys all whistle and cheer. Mark colours. But the others fall back, giving her the space she needs.

"How's things?" Mark says.

"To hell with that. I want to know what's going on," says Caz.

"Going on? What do you mean by 'going on'?"

Caz folds her arms. "You know exactly what I mean."

Mark folds his arms and tries to imitate her voice, but his mimicry is too high and squeaky to be funny. "I don't know *exactly what you mean.*"

"You've been going to Corky's church. You took Conrad and the other lads down there. What's it all about?"

"Oh, that! Maybe I've got the shaky religion."

"No, Mark. You're not the shaky-religion type. You might have taken in Neville—"

"Oh, *Neville,* is it!"

"You might have taken in Neville Corkhill, but I know you're up to something."

Mark suddenly stops his larking and becomes serious. "So you want to know what it's about, do you?"

"Of course."

"You want me to tell you what I get up to when you won't tell me what you get up to, is that it?"

Caz is stumped for a reply. There are things she's kept secret from Mark even when he's tried to help her. He's right. Why should he tell her anything? What right has she even got to ask?

"Look," says Caz. "If it's all some game to make Corky look a fool, I want to protect him. He's really not so bad. I hope you're not messing him about."

Mark shakes his head. "All right. If you want to know what it's all about, wait for me by the gates after school."

"Why? What for?"

Mark is already walking away. "School gates."

The day passes slowly. A double lesson in Maths grinds along. Caz looks up at Neville from time to time, wondering if and how he might be involved. She really hopes he's not going to be upset by whatever prank Mark is up to. In Caz's mind, Neville has gone from geek guy to decent guy, but she still somehow feels he needs protecting.

When the school day is over, she finds not only Mark and Conrad waiting for her at the school gates, but Lucy, too. She's about to demand an explanation, but Mark says, "We're just waiting for someone . . . ah, here he comes."

It's Luke Prospect, the Most Bullied Boy in the School, the kid that Mark stood up for when Caz first noticed him. Luke arrives looking rather nervous. He has his satchel carried like a backpack. He digs his thumbs under the straps as he surveys the group, eyes bulging inside the thick glass of his spectacles.

"Come on, Luke. It's all arranged."

"How long is this going to take?" Luke says suspiciously.

Caz looks at Lucy for an explanation.

"You'll see soon enough," is all she'll say.

It's about ten minutes' walk before they arrive at the wooden building of the Free Movement Ecstatic Church.

"We're not going in there," says Caz.

"Oh, yes we are," says Mark. "I've made a special appointment."

"You haven't dragged Neville Corkhill here!"

"I told you: this has nothing to do with Corky. We're meeting someone else here. Someone you know."

"Yeah," says Lucy. "He might recognise you. So you might want to wear these just in case." She hands Caz a pair of dark glasses and a headscarf.

"I'm not wearing a headscarf!" Caz protests.

"Just put it on," Lucy says, "before I slap you."

"Are you sure this is a good idea?" Luke Prospect says. He's looking up and down the street, as if thinking about making a run for it.

"Won't hurt a bit," says Conrad. "I had it done. Lucy's had it done. We've all had it done. You'll be in and out in under a minute."

"I don't know about this," Luke mutters.

Mark puts his hand on Luke's shoulder. "This is for Caz. I've explained it all to you. And remember, you do owe me one."

Luke sighs and hitches his satchel higher up his back. "Okay, let's get it over with."

Led by Mark, they enter the church. When Caz was here last, the room was loud with people "talking in tongues," as Neville described it. Now it is silent and empty, except for one man in a green suit sitting patiently on a hard chair at the far end of the room, as if expecting them.

"Ah, brought me another one, have you?" says Elder Collins in a voice that booms around the empty church.

"Yes, Elder Collins," says Mark.

Caz shrinks behind the group, afraid that Elder Collins might see through her dark glasses and headscarf.

Collins stands up, an imposing figure, his arms hanging loosely at his sides. "Another one of your Ouija-board group, is it?"

"What's that?" hisses Luke.

Conrad treads on Luke's toe as Mark says, "That's right, Elder Collins. He's afraid he might have made a mistake, too, messing around with Ouija boards. He's hoping you'll help him."

"Well, step forward, young man. Let's have a look at you."

Luke doesn't step forward. He has to be pushed to the front. Digging his thumbs under his satchel straps, he inches towards the church Elder. Collins himself takes a step forward.

"Come on, come forward. What's your name, son?"

Luke can barely croak his own name.

"Luke. A fine name. 'Bring in hither the poor, and the maimed, and the halt, and the blind.'"

"Eh?" says Luke.

"Stand up tall. Let me look at you."

Collins stares hard into Luke's eyes. His nostrils

twitch. He sniffs. He walks slowly around Luke, his nostrils twitching and sniffing all the time, as if he can smell something of the farmyard on Luke. Then he returns to his original position, slowly raising his hand just above Luke's head.

"Oh, yes indeed," booms Elder Collins, "I fear that brother Luke here has also strayed into a very dark place. Luckily for him he can join us here in the light of our church. Because . . . I . . . smell . . . *demons*!"

Collins presses his thumb hard on Luke's head. There is a hissing sound, which may come from Collins's mouth, and he jerks back his thumb as if his fingerprints have been burned off.

"Ouch!" says Luke lamely.

"On your knees, brother Luke! On your knees!"

Luke instantly does as he's told, falling to his knees, until Mark steps in and lifts him to his feet.

"Get up, Luke," Mark says. "You don't have to do that."

"What?" roars Elder Collins, taken aback by Mark's intervention.

"The thing is, Elder Collins," says Mark boldly, "that you've told all of us here that we're possessed by demons. And that business about the Ouija board, I made that up. I think you say it to everyone, just to scare people. That's why we brought Luke here. See, he's the mildest person in our school. Wouldn't say boo to a goose. Not only that, but he goes to Bible-studies class once a week at another church down the road. So it seems to me, Elder Collins, that *you* are the one possessed by all this stupidity about demons."

Collins's face is purple with rage. "You cheeky little sod!" he roars.

Then Luke speaks up. "Yes, and I know another quotation from Luke, Chapter four verse twenty-three," he gulps. *"Physician, heal thyself."*

"Get out of here!" Collins takes a step towards them.

"Look out," shouts Mark. "Elder Collins is possessed! Run!"

Caz, Lucy, Conrad, Luke, and Mark turn on their heels and clatter for the exit, letting the church door slam behind them.

They keep running until they've put a couple of hundred yards between themselves and the Free Movement Ecstatic Church. Then they collapse on each other giggling, gasping for breath, hugging their lung-cracked ribs.

"But why?" says Caz, recovering her breath.

Mark is still bent double, holding his knees. "To prove a point."

"He did it for you, you idiot," says Lucy. "To show you're not possessed after all."

"Is that true, Mark?"

Mark stands up. "I could see how upset you were after Collins had put it in your head that you were possessed by a demon. You were behaving like you believed him. So one by one we went to the church and he said exactly the same thing to all of us. So I thought if you saw him saying it to Luke here, you'd see what a fraud he is."

Caz takes off her dark glasses and her headscarf and looks at Luke, as if for confirmation of the story.

"Can I go now?" says Luke.

And for reasons no one understands, they all howl with laughter.

CHAPTER TWENTY-FIVE
We Knew That Anyway

"SAY THAT AGAIN." Caz can't believe her ears.

"Lucy can move in with us." Helen is stuffing laundry into the washing machine when she says this.

"Live here, you mean? With us? Together? All of us?"

Neville waits by the doorway, listening to the conversation, leaning against the doorframe. Caz looks at him as if she wants him to confirm what her mother has just said. He's wearing one of those thick, cable-knit white sweaters favoured by folk singers. He smiles at Caz.

"I talked about it with Neville," says Helen. "Even though it puts our own plans on hold, he thought it would be the right thing to do."

"What plans?" says Caz, looking from one to the other.

"Well," says Neville, "you know I've got this huge house on the other side of the park . . ."

"Yes?"

"Well, I asked your mum to move in with me. And she said yes—"

"She said *what*?"

"Let me finish, Caroline! She said yes if you were in agreement with that. But we hadn't had time to ask you before you mentioned Lucy and what she is going through. And right now I think Lucy needs a decent family even more than I do."

Caz stares at him. And she really can see straight into his heart. He's telling the truth. He does want a "family," and by this he means Caz and Helen. And he means what he says about Lucy. He's putting Lucy's interests first.

With a sudden stab of remorse, Caz can *see* how unfair she's been to Neville all along. He really is the sort of person who can consider another person's happiness before his own. It's almost a shock for her to recognise it. It's a true moment of growing up. "I don't know what to say!" Caz splutters.

"Don't say anything to her just yet," says Helen. "There's a lot to sort out. Her parents will have to agree. We'll have to inform the school."

"It will give her a chance at school, too," says Neville. "If she's getting knocked about at home, then she'll leave at the first opportunity, and that means she'll leave school. She's a clever girl. She can do better than she does."

And while he talks away, Caz looks at him, this sandy-haired religious nutter in his cable-knit sweater. And while he's still talking, Caz squeals with pleasure, runs at him and hugs him, burying her face in his awful sweater.

And when she at last pulls out of his cable-knit, she sees he's red in the face, embarrassed, looking at Helen, unsure what to do. But she knows he's happy, because it's the first time she's hugged him. And Caz knows that Helen is happy, too.

Over tea, they make plans about how they are going to invite Lucy to stay with them, about how they will put it to Lucy's parents, and about how the girls will be expected to contribute to the household chores. Caz feels they really are treating her as an equal partner in the discussions.

She wonders if Lucy's parents might not allow it. Neville says that if they don't, he'll bring up the issue of violence and mention the social services and the police to them. Caz knows he means it. Not so soft, after all.

Neville makes her another promise: that he will never try to stuff his religion down her throat ever again. He tells her he's learned his lesson. He's also got something to report about Elder Collins at the church. It seems that Collins has "retired."

"Oh, why's that?" Helen wants to know.

"Some incident down at the church the other day," Neville says, glancing at Caz. "It seems he's something of a fraud."

Helen sniffs with satisfaction. "Well, we knew that anyway, didn't we, Caroline?"

That night Caz lies awake thinking about the implications of Lucy coming to live with them. A beam of moonlight, entering her room through a crack in the curtains, spotlights the wardrobe door. The light is keeping her awake. She knows she should get up and close the curtains properly, but she's too cosy in her bed. Her mind flies back, as it often does, to the night she did the Creepy Thing with Lucy. She wonders what might have happened if Lucy had been the one to have had the bracelet clamped on her wrist by Mrs Tranter. She wonders how things might have worked out differently.

And as she stares up into the grey light of the softly moonlit room, the wardrobe door slowly begins to open. A brilliant light starts to bleed at the edge of the opening door, acid and foamy light, bubbling like spit on a griddle. Caz is astonished. She kneels upright in her bed, her hands over her mouth. Because there behind the light is the woman Fizz. She has her dark glasses in her hands and Caz is certain now that the weird light is coming not from the wardrobe but from the woman. Fizz shapes her mouth to speak to Caz, but instead of words coming from her mouth there is more foaming light. Fear: Caz can taste it in her mouth. The bubbling light forms itself into worms, which in turn take the shape of letters: *Accept*. Then, like a bulb in a lamp expiring without warning, the frothing light is gone, leaving the wardrobe door hanging open and lit only by the thin stream of moonlight coming in at the curtains.

Caz realises she has her jaws clenched together. She

breathes again. Slowly her heart rate begins to return to normal.

With trembling fingers she switches on her bedside reading lamp. She gets up and goes to the wardrobe, still half expecting Fizz to jump out at her, but although the wardrobe door is open, there is no sign of anything unusual. Caz wonders if she had been on the verge of falling asleep: maybe she's dreaming these things.

But no. She knows too well it's no dream. She was—and is—wide awake.

Inside the wardrobe the pile of comics has slipped, just as before, toppling onto the door, pushing it out. There's always a reason for these things: it explains how the door came to come open again. Or it would do, except for the fact that Caz knows perfectly well that she always keeps the wardrobe door securely locked.

She tries the key. It locks the wardrobe door efficiently. She unlocks it again.

Caz bends down to tidy the spilled pile of comics. Then she has second thoughts, deciding that maybe it's time to throw this pile of old junk away, especially if it's taking up too much room in her wardrobe.

She carries a pile of comics and dumps them on her table to be discarded in the morning. She goes back to get more, but as she places this second pile of comics on the table, the bold colour cover of the top copy catches her eye.

It's an American superhero comic. The title of the comic asks: FRIEND OR FOE? The superhero is toppling from a tall building. A female figure is either grabbing him by the wrist to save him or pushing him to his doom.

Caz is on her knees, staring at the comic in her hands, the words lit by the weak light coming from her bedside table. The female figure in the cover drawing wears black clothes, dark glasses, and gothlike swept-back hair.

The figure in the cover artwork is Fizz.

On Wednesday night Caz goes to work at The Black Dog. She's still trying to puzzle out the connection between the comic and the figure of the woman who keeps appearing to her. So far all she has is this: Fizz is the name of the woman in the comic. Of course she remembered it when she saw it, even though it must have been a few years since she'd last read it. She just doesn't know how she's managed to make Fizz appear in real life.

If that's what she's doing.

"You're two minutes and thirty-five seconds late," Frank growls when she gets to the pub. "Get to work."

Caz has learned to smile at this. Even though Frank never cracks a smile over it himself. It's just not his way.

"That's all right," Lucy shouts from behind the bar, "'Cos I was three minutes early, so Caz can have that time."

Frank turns to Lucy. "And as for you—"

But he doesn't get time to finish what he's saying, because Caz grabs Lucy's arm and whisks her away to the bottle room. "Come on, I've got something to tell you."

Helen and Neville have agreed that Caz should make the offer to Lucy, and here she is. Lucy listens, wide-eyed at this proposal.

"Sure," says Lucy. "Would be good."

"Is that it?" says Caz.

"What do you mean is that it? It would be great. Yes, I'd like to. Do you want me to fall on the floor and kiss your feet and say thank you for saving me? Sure, I'll move in."

Caz stares in disbelief. Then once again she sees behind Lucy's bravado. She sees behind her cool. She sees that Lucy can't gush and cry and admit how badly she would like to get away from her home. It is only by being tough and strong and not crying that she's managed to get through the kickings and the bruisings. It would be a weakness. It would invite more kickings and bruisings. Sometimes Caz marvels at this new skill she has. Sometimes it actually hurts her. *How did it ever become a crime to admit to a weakness?* she thinks. *Why does this shame have to make us so damned hard?* She wants to cuddle Lucy. But she knows that right now that's the very last thing Lucy wants.

That's the other part of the special insight she's been granted: the ability to know when to speak and when to stay silent. So she says, "We just have to get permission from your own mum and dad."

"It's done."

"Huh?"

"I already asked them. I told you: they don't really care. They said it would be fine."

"So did you already know that my mum would say that you could come and live with us?"

"No. I just hoped she would." Lucy smiles a very thin smile. And in that thin smile Caz sees how desperately Lucy wants it to happen.

Frank appears at the door. "What's this? The knitting

circle? The village youth club? I don't pay you to hang out and spend the night yakking, you know. Let's get some bloody work done round here."

He turns to go but Caz calls him back. "Frank. This is really important girls' talk. So stop going round like a grumpy old bear with a sore head, okay?"

Frank stops midstride. Turns round. Lifts a finger in the air and opens his mouth. But nothing comes out. His finger is wagging in the air, bouncing back and forth, but for once Frank is speechless. Maybe he's not accustomed to being answered back, but he just can't find any words. Caz and Lucy cant their heads to one side, eyes opened wide in mockery, waiting for him to say something, knowing he won't.

The moment is saved for Frank when Liz the barmaid appears. "There's a kid here from a band who wants to see you."

Liz steps aside and lets the kid through. Caz recognises him instantly. He's the drummer from the band that Frank slung out of the pub several nights ago. Frank doesn't recognise him quite so quickly.

Then the penny drops for Frank. "What the hell do you want? Get out of here, you Muppet."

The young man colours up. He's got Liz, Lucy, and Caz watching him, and he's about to beg. "I wanted to ask you for another gig."

"Ha! Great sense of humour, kiddiwinks!" Frank jerks a thumb over his shoulder. "If I want to listen to metal being smacked around, I'll go to the car crusher. Now sling your hook somewhere else."

"Hear me out: we dumped our singer 'cos he was bad.

And we've tightened up. Getting thrown out that night did us some good. We've rehearsed every night. We're tighter and we've got a keyboard man who can really play. Give us another chance."

"On yer bike, son." Frank turns his back on the young man, who looks crestfallen.

"Wait a minute, Frank," says Caz. "Maybe the guys really have learned their lesson."

"Huh?" goes Frank.

"I mean," Caz continues, "everyone deserves a second chance, don't they? Everyone."

Frank blinks at Caz. Then he turns round and stares hard at the young musician. And blinks at him, too.

The boy shuffles his feet. No one is saying anything.

Finally the youth says, "Does that mean we get a second chance?"

"Apparently," says Frank.

"Really? We get to try again?"

"Apparently."

"Yes! We won't let you down."

"See if you can find them a Wednesday booking," Frank says to Liz.

Liz laughs. "She's got you round her little finger, hasn't she!"

"Apparently," Frank growls. "Now can we get some sodding *work* done around here?"

CHAPTER TWENTY-SIX
Don't Look Back

NEVILLE HAS HIRED a van to collect Lucy's things. They're going to bring her bed and her wardrobe, plus all her clothes and other stuff over to Caz's house. Caz sits up front with Neville as he crunches through the unfamiliar gears at traffic lights, laughing at the grinding gearbox.

"Well, I'll get to meet Lucy's parents," Neville says.

"Bet you won't."

"Why not?"

"Bet you anything they're not there."

They drive awhile in silence. Then Neville asks Caz about what happened with Elder Collins at the church. Caz tells him straight up. He laughs when Caz tells her about Luke quoting the Bible right back at Collins. Then he frowns. "I'm sorry about putting you through all that."

"Forget it," Caz says. "I have."

The silence is uncomfortable, so Caz says, "What's your favourite bit in the Bible?"

"Oh, there's hundreds. But in Luke, the bit you're talking about, it would be: 'No one, having lighted a candle, puts it in a secret place or under a bushel.'"

"Heck! What does that mean?"

"Well, a bushel is just a box of some kind. It means if you're given a gift—and my gift seems to be teaching—then you should use it and not hide it away."

Could that refer to her, too? To what she has seen as a curse? Caz is struck dumb for a moment.

"You okay?"

"Yeah," Caz says. "Yeah."

"Good, because here we are."

Lucy is waiting for them, and everything is ready to be carried out to the hired van. Caz was spot-on; Lucy's parents are nowhere around. Caz knows the reason for this: they can't look Neville in the eye. They will probably have guessed that he knows some of what has gone on there. Caz says nothing about this, and neither does Lucy.

Together the three of them make quick work of hauling out Lucy's things. While they are doing so, Caz checks out the house. It's ordinary in every sense: neat and tidy with nice carpets and sofas and curtains. Close the doors and there is nothing to tell you that a little girl has been kicked black and blue for ten years without anybody ever lifting a finger to stop it.

When they are done, Lucy closes the door behind her, walks up the path, and gets into the van. She could be going to the cinema, not leaving home. She doesn't even look back.

That afternoon the girls have great fun setting up Lucy's room. Caz's mum has been shopping for a new duvet set, and Caz has bought her a cool clock radio to set by her bed. They cover the walls in posters. They eat pizza in the room. They try on each other's clothes. Caz knows that Lucy is unbelievably happy; she also knows that Lucy is afraid it might not last, and that she might be sent home.

So she says: "My mum says you can stay for as long as you feel okay here. It's really up to you. You don't have to leave unless you want to."

Caz can see that Lucy's eyes are filling up. Lucy turns away and puts something loud on her CD player. Then she drops the volume, out of consideration for Caz's mum.

Caz just knows it's going to be fine.

They stay up late that night, in their pyjamas, in Lucy's new room. They talk about how things might work out with this new arrangement. They talk about school, about Frank at the pub, about Mark and Conrad—they talk about everything. Everything except Caz's mysterious tattoo and the missing bracelet.

For some reason they stay off that subject. Though Caz knows it is on Lucy's mind almost as much as it is on her own. For Lucy, it's like not talking about her bruises. It's a subject to be avoided: don't go touching wounds. But Caz can see that Lucy has indeed got something to say about it. She thinks that Lucy will speak when she's good and ready.

Some time after midnight Lucy falls asleep on her bed, almost in the middle of a conversation. It's been an exhausting day. Caz covers her with her new duvet, turns off the light, and returns to her own room.

Something is bothering Caz as she pulls back her own duvet covers and climbs into bed. She looks at her wrist. The tattoo has almost completely faded. It's there but you have to focus steadily to actually see it at all. A casual glance would miss it. She switches off the light.

No one who has lighted a candle puts it in a secret place.

It's spooky how that phrase has been running round her head all day. She lies in bed, turning it over, chasing its meaning.

Caz is almost falling asleep when she sees the light begin to form around the wardrobe door all over again. A thread of white light, growing fatter at the door hinges. She closes her eyes because she doesn't want to see it, but when she opens them again, it's still there, and now the door has swung open again, very slightly. She would go and slam the door shut, but she's too frightened.

Slowly the door opens and the white, frothing light thickens.

This time there is no pile of comics to push open the door. It's no surprise this time when the woman herself appears. It's Fizz, and though terrified by her, Caz has been expecting her. She's wearing dark glasses and the sodium light is hissing behind the shades.

Trembling, Caz barely manages to speak. "Who? What?"

The woman opens her mouth to answer, but only that same milky white frothing and fizzing light comes out. Caz knows that Fizz is trying to speak but finding it hard. Then once again the light turns itself into words: words that Caz can *see* instead of *hear,* maybe in the same way that you read the words of a character in a comic, but with no speech balloons to hold them in place so the words go twisting and snaking around the room, smoky, breaking up here and there. Caz catches only some of it.

"I'm that part of you . . ." Fizz is saying. "The part of you that you needed to help yourself. When you took on the bracelet . . . you had to call on the strongest part of you."

"But you stepped out of the comic . . . ?" Caz doesn't know if she's just thinking this, or speaking aloud.

"No. I'm from your memory of that comic. You needed me. I came. And now you don't need me anymore. That's good."

"But I do need you! I have to get rid of the bracelet! Like Mrs Tranter!"

"She wasn't ready for it. You are. You've already started helping people, which is something she couldn't do. She had this for fifty years and in all that time she didn't learn a single thing from it. You've already grown beyond her. Accept it, Caz. *Accept it.*"

"I don't understand any of this!"

"You will. I came here to say good-bye."

Fizz extends a hand to touch Caroline on the wrist, but as soon as her finger strokes the faint tattoo there, something happens. It's exactly like the moment in the tattoo parlour, when the laser light comes into contact with Caz's skin. There is a sudden loss of power, a drop in energy, a feeling like a machine just shut down, even though there is no machine.

Fizz is gone.

Caz is left with her hand reaching out to touch empty space.

Then she sees someone standing in the doorway. It's Lucy, rubbing sleep from her eyes, blinking at her.

"I heard voices," says Lucy. "Who are you talking to?"

"Did you see her? She was here!"

"Who?" Lucy says. "Who was here?"

Caz collapses back on her bed. She thinks she may be going mad. But then she sees that Lucy is pointing at something.

"Look!" says Lucy.

"What?"

Caz's eyes track to where Lucy is pointing. It's the bracelet. It is back on Caz's wrist. And it is glowing in the colours of her tattoo.

"Is this it? Is this *the* bracelet?" Lucy's voice is almost hoarse.

Caz touches the bracelet. The clasp flies open.

Lucy shoots out her arm. "Put it on me," she says.

"No!"

"I've thought about this, Caz. It was my fault! I dared you to do the Creepy Thing in the first place. It was me who led you there. It was my stupidity. I was daring you all the time. And all you ever gave me back was friendship. Loads of times I've thought that if I could take the thing off you I would. Put it on me!"

Caz slides the bracelet along her arm. "You'd really take all this trouble off me and put it on yourself?"

"Here's my arm."

Caz fumbles with the bracelet, then stops. "I can't do that to you, Lucy. It's a curse. I wouldn't do that to you."

"Put it on me!"

Caz shakes her head. Lucy makes a grab for the bracelet, but Caz locks the clasp shut again. There is a moment of chill in her heart when she knows she might have locked herself alone with the bracelet all over again.

Lucy sighs, defeated.

Caz checks the clasp and finds that this time she can open and close the bracelet easily. She closes it and opens it. Closes it and opens it. "No, Lucy. I've already figured out what I'm going to do."

CHAPTER TWENTY-SEVEN

Not from a Boy

CAZ AND LUCY are lolling on Caz's bed, talking. It's their first weekend together, and they can't seem to stop talking.

Helen opens the bedroom door. "It's nearly the middle of the day and look at you two! Get dressed, why don't you?"

Caz yawns, Lucy blinks.

"Come on," says Helen. "Neville will be here in a few minutes. He doesn't want to see you two half undressed."

"Let him look," says Lucy.

"Ugh," says Caz. "You tart."

"You trollop."

"You slut."

"You slattern."

"You Jezebel."

"You—"

"Oh, for heaven's sake!" shouts Helen, leaving the room. "Just get dressed."

Caz throws a pillow at Lucy.

When they are dressed, Lucy has a plan. She wants to text Mark so that he and Conrad and the two of them can get together. "You game?" asks Lucy, already keying the message before she's answered.

"Sure."

"Not *busy* this afternoon?" Caz has told Lucy the full story about her errands for Mrs Tranter.

"No, not busy."

A message comes back in under a minute. It turns out he and Conrad are free. They suggest meeting in the park and then maybe a trip to the cinema afterwards. Caz suspects that Lucy has stitched this meeting up all along. A meeting time of two o'clock is suggested.

"Make it three thirty," says Caz.

Lucy sends her message. It's fixed. She flips her phone shut. "Why later?"

"I've got one errand to do first. You're coming with me."

"Have I got time to do my eyelashes?"

"Tart!"

"Slut!"

"Oh, no," says Lucy. "I'm not going in there. I thought you said you were finished with her."

They are outside the gate to number 13 Briar Street. Lucy has never been back here since the fateful night of the Creepy.

"It's okay. We're not going inside. There's just one thing I need to do."

Caz opens the gate, which she notes is new, and steps up to the door. Lucy hangs back a few paces as Caz presses the doorbell. After a few moments the shuffling figure of Mrs Tranter can be made out behind the frosted glass. The door opens just a crack.

"Oh, it's you," says the old woman. "I knew as you'd be back. Didn't I say it? And who's this you've brought with you?"

"Just a friend."

"Is she a better worker than you are? Come in. There's painting to be done and I've run out of money. I want my kitchen floor scrubbed."

"No, Mrs Tranter, I'm not scrubbing your floor today. I'm going to the shops. I've just come to see if you want anything picked up."

"Shops? I don't want no shopping! I want my floor cleaning and one or two other jobs a-doing."

"Okay, bye then," Caz says, stepping back. "I'm offering to do a bit of shopping for you, that's all. But if you don't want anything . . ."

"Wait! Wait. If you're too bone idle to do anything other, then there are one or two things you can get me from the shops. Wait there and I'll make out a shopping list."

The old woman leaves the door ajar. Caz turns to Lucy, who shakes her head, a quizzical expression on her face. She can't understand what Caz is up to.

After a while Mrs Tranter comes back with a list of groceries, parting with it as if she is doing Caz a big favour. She hands Caz a twenty-pound note. "And I want the change out of that."

Caz takes the list. "I'll bring the shopping back just after three."

"But I gets my hair permed at three! You should know that! You should know I always go out at three!"

Caz does indeed know that. Mrs Tranter *always* has a Saturday-afternoon appointment at three, either at the hairdressers, the chiropodist, the local palm reader, or just to feed the pigeons in the park. How could Caz possibly forget?

"Oh, of course. You'll have to give me the spare key and I'll drop the groceries off while you're out."

Mrs Tranter goes away muttering and returns with the spare key. She looks sharply at Lucy. "Have I seen you somewhere before?"

"No!" Lucy says, too quickly and too loud.

"Bye," says Caz, already halfway down the path. Lucy hurries to her side.

"She gives me the creeps," Lucy says as they walk to the shops.

"She's lost the talent. Now that she doesn't have the bracelet, it's gone."

"What?"

"The talent to see through people. I needed to know. She's lost it."

"What are you up to, Caz?"

They complete the shopping for Mrs Tranter. Most of it they pick up from the supermarket, the baker's, and the pharmacy. Near the supermarket is a hardware shop. Caz tells Lucy to wait outside with the shopping while she gets the last thing on her list. When Caz has everything, they return to Mrs Tranter's house, by which time the old lady is out.

Lucy still refuses to come inside, preferring to wait by the gate. Caz uses the spare key to let herself in. Once inside she unpacks the groceries in the kitchen and leaves Mrs Tranter's change and her spare key on the kitchen table.

Then she's out of there, and on her way, with Lucy, to meet Mark and Conrad in the park.

It's a glorious afternoon. The giant cedar trees in the park send long, rich shadows across the grass, and swans glide on the river. The four of them fool around on the grassy banks by the castle ruins. At some point in the afternoon, Caz looks up and sees Lucy and Conrad play-fighting and it ends with them snogging.

Sunlight spills through the trees like honey. Mark squints at Caz, and then he kisses her, and it seems like the golden light is flaking on his lips. Caz puts her tongue in his mouth. He tastes of sunlight and honey.

When they stop kissing, Mark says, "Where did the bracelet come from?"

Caz fingers the bracelet. "It was a gift."

"From a boy?"

"No, not from a boy."

"Are we going out together again, Caz?"

Caz looks up at the sky before looking back at him. "I'd say it looks like it."

"Yeah. Looks like it."

Caz sighs and calls across to Lucy. It's late and they have to go home and prepare for work at The Black Dog.

Marks frowns. "Do you absolutely *have* to work there?"

"No. Not anymore. But I kind of like it."

"Okay, I'll let you go if you promise to see me tomorrow."

"We can spend all day together tomorrow if you want."

"All day?"

"Remember when I asked you to meet me really late, at the bandstand one night?"

"Yeah. I never showed up."

"Neither did I. What if I said I'd meet you tomorrow, but really early instead of really late? Like eight o'clock in the morning."

"Eight in the morning? You're crazy! Why?"

"Don't ask why. Yes or no. At the bandstand."

"Okay, yes."

"Yay! Now I have to go." Caz stands up, brushing grass from her clothes. "Lucy, you tart! Get that boy's tongue out of your mouth!"

CHAPTER TWENTY-EIGHT
The Biggest Question of All

CAZ IS ALREADY awake before her alarm sings out at six A.M. She stifles it quickly. She wants neither Lucy nor her mum to know that she's up and about. Mum will sleep forever anyway, and Lucy will lie in late. Caz dresses quickly and quietly.

She eats some cereal and milk for breakfast, though her stomach is rioting at what she's about to do. She has to dash to the bathroom to retch, but nothing comes. After that, she listens hard to make sure she hasn't woken the others.

She scribbles a note, which she leaves on the kitchen table: *Couldn't sleep, gone for a walk in the park, c u later x.* The time is 6:20. Caz fingers the bracelet on her wrist, takes a deep breath, then silently lets herself out of the front door, letting it close behind her with only the faintest click.

She sets off down the street. It's a beautiful morning. A light and silvery mist has risen from the river, but the sun is already busily burning it away. The air is mint-fresh and quite cool. There is very little traffic about. The milkman's float whirrs by as he makes his deliveries, bottles clinking in the crates.

It's a great day for getting rid of a bracelet.

It takes no more than fifteen minutes to get where she's going. She's given herself plenty of time, but her heart is hammering and even though the sun is not too hot, she finds she's sweating. She has to sit down at a bench at a bus stop to compose herself, to breathe steadily. She puts her head between her legs for a moment, and her desperate heart rate begins to settle.

She calculates that she's lost about five minutes doing this, but she knows she's still in good time. She's planned this over and over in her head. She's calculated the time very carefully.

As she approaches number 13 Briar Street, she looks at her watch. Twenty minutes before seven. She looks up and down the street, knowing that she mustn't hang around at the gate in a way that would arouse any suspicion. She needs to go straight up to the door.

But she can't seem to pass through the gate. The muscles in her legs feel as though they've turned to liquid. She's become paralysed. *Move, Caz,* she tells herself. *Move.*

At last she breaks out of her panic and swings open the gate. It's a new gate and its hinges make no sound: she's thankful for that. She walks quickly up the path, producing the key she had cut in the hardware store during yesterday's shopping expedition. The key trembles in her grasp, but it slides home. It turns sweetly in the barrel of the lock and the door opens. She closes the door silently behind her.

She's in.

Caz stands in the hall, waiting, straining to listen for the slightest movement from upstairs: a squeak of the bedsprings, a creak from the bed frame, the tiniest rustle of bedclothes. She listens, and the whole house listens with her. That clock in the hall ticks on heavily. It's almost a quarter to seven.

Caz breathes deep. The house is different now—different from that first time Caz came here. The dirty old carpet from underfoot has been replaced with new nylon twist, and the damp patches on the walls have been treated and painted over. Some of the painting is Caz's handiwork. The damp mould smells have gone from the place, but not the odour of potpourri nor the sweet smell of decay she has come to associate with Mrs Tranter herself.

In fact she can smell the old woman everywhere in the house. Caz's new fear is that the old woman will be able, in turn, to smell her, even in her sleep, that Caz's own scent will drift into Mrs Tranter's dreams and alert her to what is going on.

Caz steps past the wall clock, careful not to brush the aspidistra plant on the small table. She lightly sets foot on the first step.

She makes her way steadily up the stairs, trying to

remember all the creak points, and the place where the banister always groans.

Downstairs in the hall the letter flap opens, loud as a gunshot it seems. Caz freezes. Her eyes flare open with horror. The paperboy. Surely he's awoken the old lady.

Caz strains her ears to listen for any sigh or movement from the room. She hears nothing. She looks back down the stairs and can see through the frosted glass that the paperboy hasn't gone away. He's lingering at the door.

Then with mounting horror Caz realises that he's about to ring the bell.

Caz leaps back down the few stairs already ascended and slides over to the door, managing to get it open as the boy's finger hovers over the bell-push. She presses her finger against her lips. "Shhh. Aunty's sleeping," she says sweetly.

"Can't get it through the letterbox," says the boy. Mrs Tranter still thinks she's going up in the world: she's ordered a fat broadsheet. The boy grins at her, hands over the massive Sunday newspaper, and goes on his way.

Caz closes the door, breathes hard, and carefully sets the newspaper down on the table under the wall clock.

She looks at the clock. She still has time, and from upstairs there is not a stir. Caz mounts the stairs slowly, silently, all over again.

The banister creaks. Caz waits and moves on. At last she reaches Mrs Tranter's bedroom. She inches open the door. The old woman is lying on her side, just as she was that first time, with the covers pulled up to her chin. She wheezes slightly in her sleep.

The old alarm clock ticks as loudly as ever on the bedside table. Its illuminated hands point to the roman numerals: ten minutes before seven. Caz knows that at exactly seven o'clock the hammers poised at either side of the twin bells will strike, and that Mrs Tranter, still half asleep, will reach out her hand to silence the alarm. She will reach out and offer her wrist, and in that moment Caz will return the gift that was given to her.

Where on that first night Caz had to pass what seemed like a lifetime in waiting out a mere fifteen seconds, she now has ten full minutes. Caz fingers the clasp on the bracelet. It opens sweetly. When the moment comes she will grab the old woman's wrist with her left hand and snap on the bracelet with her right. She just has to wait it out.

The old woman doesn't stir. Suddenly feeling a thrill of confidence, Caz sees the hard wooden chair behind her. She lifts it and places it next to the bed without a sound before settling into it. She waits. She watches.

It's a long ten minutes. The minute hand on the clock seems to have frozen. Caz stares at the old woman's sleeping head. Mrs Tranter's chest rises and falls slightly under the bedclothes. Her breath wheezes. Caz remembers the time when she did the Creepy Thing on Mrs Tranter and thought that her breathing had stopped. That was what had made her reach out, and was the thing that allowed Mrs Tranter to clamp the bracelet on Caz's wrist. Handcuffing her to these mysterious powers.

Caz has time to think about everything that has happened in between. The tattoo, which has now completely vanished from her wrist. The laser machine at the tattoo parlour that blew up every time it came into contact with the tattoo. Elder Collins, the old fraud who made her think she was possessed by some demon from the bracelet, but who has been exposed by Mark. And then, after that, she had come to realise that Fizz, her mysterious helper, was not a demon or an "other" at all but a part of herself she had conjured from her own memories and needs buried. Though, in her way, Fizz *had* been real.

Seven minutes to go.

Caz thinks about Frank and her job at The Black Dog. She thinks about how, even though she's just a kid, she's been able to help this man, whom life had made sad. And Lucy, the friend who had led her to this house. And her mum, talking to her out of the fog of pills.

She's been helping people, and helping people has made her kinder to herself. She's older, wiser, and smarter all because of the powers that came with the bracelet. The powers Mrs Tranter calls a curse.

Five minutes.

She has time, too, to think about this so-called curse. The way it seemed to her that as soon as she'd passed on the bracelet, things started going well for Mrs Tranter and badly for Caz. But since Mark exposed Collins as a fake, Caz has stopped worrying about being possessed. She's also given up on the idea of removing her tattoo. And since she's stopped worrying, her skin cleaned up a little.

Maybe her hair wasn't really falling out at all. And as for Mrs Tranter, well, the only difference between her before the bracelet and after it was that she inherited some money from a cousin who died.

It occurs to Caz that most of these things have nothing at all to do with the bracelet. These are just things that occur in life. Stuff happens. Life happens.

Three minutes.

But changes have indeed been caused by the bracelet. The powers that come with the bracelet are very real. Caz is not going to deny that for one second. For one thing, Fizz was real, for as long as Caz needed her. For another there is the *insight*. The special gift of being able to see if someone is speaking the truth or if they are lying. But even that on its own is not the half of it. The truth thing is just the surface. See past whether they are being honest or not, and you begin to see if they are lying because they are afraid, or because they feel hurt or lonely or rejected. Knowing these things about a person changes everything.

If anyone was offered that gift—just offered it, not clamped on them with a bracelet—would they take it? It's like a choice: stay blind to what everyone else is feeling around you and carry on living and eating and drinking in a kind of half-sleep; or accept this gift, this vision, this ability to see and to sympathise and sometimes to help. Caz wonders what most people would do. Would the average person take it on?

It's a big question.

One minute.

Caz gazes at Mrs Tranter's sleeping head. Her mind empties itself of all these things as she waits for the alarm to ring. She fingers the bracelet in readiness. She stares at the sleeping figure in the bed. It occurs to her in the last fifteen seconds that she's back where she started, doing the Creepy Thing. Only this is the longest Creepy ever.

Seven o'clock. The alarm rings loud. Louder than Caz ever expected.

Mrs Tranter reaches out her bony arm to switch off the alarm clock, just as she has done every morning for so many, many years. She fumbles for the switch just as she always has done, and the bell stops, just as it always has done. Only this morning she feels Caz's hand close hard and fast over her wrist.

The old woman lifts up her head, still trying to wake. It's like watching a swimmer come to the surface from beneath the waves. She squints at Caz. Then her eyes fill with terror as she quickly takes in the situation. She sees the gleaming silver bracelet in Caz's other hand, at the ready. She tries to drag back her wrist, but Caz has a firm grip.

"What are you doing in my house?" she croaks.

"I've come to return a gift," Caz says.

The old woman whimpers. She knows she's lost.

"I wanted to show you," Caz says, "that I could give it back to you. That I could always find a way."

She releases the old woman's wrist. Mrs Tranter, shivering, still whimpering, her mouth working like that of a fish in a bowl, huddles back against the headboard of her bed.

"You can stop making that noise. I'm going to keep the bracelet."

"You're not—"

"No, I'm not putting it back on you." Caz waves the bracelet at her. "The thing is, Mrs Tranter, you had something very special for fifty years. And in all those fifty years you were too selfish to realise how beautiful that thing is. You weren't ready for it. You weren't worthy of it."

Mrs Tranter watches her with big round suspicious eyes.

"I've found out everything I need to know," says Caz. "You see, Mrs Tranter, now I know more than you do."

Caz stands up. She clips the bracelet back on her own wrist. The clasp closes with a tiny click. Caz turns to leave the room.

Mrs Tranter recovers. "You'll come to no good, you will! I'll tell the police you've been here, I will! And what about these walls! You haven't finished painting them!"

Caz laughs. "Good-bye, Mrs Tranter."

Caz walks calmly downstairs. Behind her she can hear Mrs Tranter shrieking and trying to get dressed. Downstairs, she leaves behind the key she had cut and lets herself out.

She knows that number 13 Briar Street will not trouble her again.

It's a beautiful morning. The air is still mint-fresh and the sun has burned away the morning mist. A sweet breeze blows in from the river. It's still early, but a few more people are about. Walking to the park, Caz feels light. She feels like she could float. She feels like singing.

She follows the course of the river through the park, then makes her away across the grassy bank towards the bandstand. When she looks up, she sees that Mark is waiting for her. He waves. She waves back happily, and for a moment her silver bracelet gleams with brilliant, reflected light.

GRAHAM JOYCE is the author of thirteen novels and has won numerous awards for his writing, including four British Fantasy Awards and the 2003 World Fantasy Award for *The Facts of Life.* He has worked as a teacher, and spent eight years working for a youth organization. He currently teaches creative writing at Nottingham Trent University, and lives in Leicester with his wife and their two children.

Visit his Web site at www.grahamjoyce.net.